BEYOND THE HEADLINES

TRUE CRIME'S MYTHS AND LEGENDS

SERIAL KILLERS | VOLUME ONE

JEFF IGNATOWSKI

WILD BLUE PRESS

WildBluePress.com

BEYOND THE HEADLINES

CONTENTS

PREFACE

True Crime has been a part of my life for as long as I can remember. I grew up right outside Philadelphia in a time when the Mafia subculture was admired and emulated. It didn't help that, through marriage, we had a whole side of the family that was Italian. I had an uncle Primo and Sonny, you don't get much more Italian than that. They also owned businesses that were fronts for the mob before I was born, so as a child I heard all the stories.

Although I am Filipino, Polish, and German, I grew up fully in the mythology of the ethical mafioso and the need to always take care of "family." We always wanted to be a part of the mob, even though we knew we could never be part of it. My dad was friends with several people in the Philadelphia mob and would tell me stories of sit-downs with Angelo Bruno, the final one a few weeks before Angelo was gunned down.

From an early age, I would hear the story of my dad meeting Charles Manson in the early 1960s. This was a few years before the Manson murders and Manson was not interested in my dad taking part in any of their festivities. My dad and his friend would eventually decide to go back and attempt to rob Manson of his drugs; however, they were unable to find the party. This would be the story that really fueled my interest in true crime. I wanted to understand all these people whom I found so fascinating. Why did they do what they did? How did they become who they became?

What were the circumstances that allowed them to continue to commit these crimes?

These questions are the ones that so many people have pondered and will continue to ponder. If you have had an opportunity to hear me speak you already know that I approach this subject from a unique perspective. I have not only been fascinated by these questions, but I've also struggled with many of the circumstances that these killers have faced. I fit all of the qualifications of the MacDonald Triad (formerly believed to be the indicator of a killer, now just violent behavior). I also have struggled, most of my life, with the intrusive thoughts that many of our killers have dealt with. So, the additional question that I've always asked myself is, why not me?

Why do some people decide to kill and follow through with it? Why do others, with similar backgrounds, influences, and experiences decide to not give in to their darker desires? Why do our darker desires often lead us into our own personal struggles with either rage, anxiety, or depression? The experiences that we gather through this trip called life give us a distinct perspective. There may be means of approach similar to others, but your life will always be yours and yours alone. This point of view, when shared, can enrich all of us and bring us closer to true understanding. As you read this book, I hope that my point of view will inspire you to search deeper, further, and give you the willingness to share your viewpoint with the rest of us.

As I have traveled around the country, I often hear many stories about people's personal experiences with true crime. Enthralled, I am always trying to understand how they have related to those events and engaged with the darkness. What I find is that there are three kinds of people. There are those that stay in the shallow end, close to the shore, believing that it will keep them safe. Others swim around a little, just enjoying the water, confident that they are getting just enough. Then there are those that throw caution to the wind and dive right into the deep waters, searching for all that they can find. I hope you will join me, and dive...

Into the deep waters…

Jeff Ignatowski
Owner of Scorpion Lair Games

FOREWORD

When Jeff Ignatowski approached me to write the foreword for his book, I was both honored and excited. To be able to introduce this audience to the expansive knowledge of my friend and colleague is a real pleasure. From the moment I met Jeff, his interest in true crime was obvious. It's not just because he was wearing a hat with a man's facial skin on it! Anyone who can hold his own in a conversation with me about serial killers knows a great deal and has deep insight into their machinations. It doesn't hurt that Jeff's penchant for digging beneath the surface of any criminal's modus operandi knows no bounds. I've had the pleasure of getting to know him over the past couple of years and I've learned that he has a knack for cutting through the bullshit and baring the truth, no matter how ugly.

In this book, you'll explore various myths and legends about infamous and lesser-known serial killers through the well-reasoned eyes of a serial killer expert. Jeff seeks to diffuse the larger-than-life celebrity status garnered by most criminals by the media and the well-meaning public. He provides detailed information about each subject and distills the data into easy-to-read sections. He's highly skilled at revealing the motivations of various serial killers and understanding the criminal mindset. When we discussed his plans for this book, I was truly impressed with his vision. The true crime genre includes various anthologies, but most of them simply summarize information about each killer and leave it at that. Here you'll read the briefest of synopses before you get to the heart of each account. The myths and legends surrounding each killer are well-researched and provide new ways of seeing the truth beyond the fiction.

The time and energy put into this volume have yielded a vast collection of details that have up until now been overlooked and discounted. Jeff takes us through many of the popular opinions related to each killer and shines a light on the reality of each individual. If there's one true crime book this year that will take the world by storm, you're reading it! Now sit back, relax, and prepare to be educated.

E.J. Hammon
True Crime Author and Historian

INTRODUCTION

There are so many books out there about true crime, why do we need another? Many of them tell the story of a specific killer or crime, while others focus on a specific aspect of the account. This book incorporates a different mindset on the topic of true crime. There are sociological effects that our consumption of true crime has on our culture that impact society. With that in mind, the myths and legends that have arisen from our favorite true crime stories have a significant impact on us. They cause us to clutch our purse when we get the "uh oh" feeling from someone or lock our doors in a bad neighborhood. This book's intention is to lay the groundwork for further study and contemplation. It is important to take an objective look at our "history" and our beliefs about it to shape the way that we interact with our future. This will enable us to develop new techniques and better forensics to curb crime. The myths and legends contained within are neither true nor false, but rather a window into the mindset of the people that have believed them. In both Greek and Norse Mythology, there is an interplay between the ethics of the Gods and humans. In our own "American" cultural mythology we have taken these killers and made them both evil and anti-hero to suit our own beliefs. They often seem to have supernatural powers to remain undetected and are either hated or revered by the people who engage with them.

Before we discuss the killers, we need to define the difference between a myth and a legend. A myth is defined as a popular belief that has grown up around something or someone. For example, the myth that J. Edgar Hoover wore women's clothing. A legend is defined as a traditional story sometimes popularly regarded as historical but unauthenticated. As in the legend of Paul Revere, that often is intertwined with the legend of Sleepy Hollow.

I started this journey with the mindset to write one book in three parts. Part 1 would be about serial killers, Part 2 about criminals, and Part 3 would focus on cults and religion. As you can tell, I started writing and found that I needed to split it up into three volumes rather than parts. I didn't want to release an 800-page tome about true crime. For those of you who have heard me speak, you know I can be a bit long-winded. So I should have known that this endeavor would take me on a much longer journey than I had anticipated. There are many myths and legends that I was unable to cover that may make an appearance in later volumes, as well as many other true crime subjects that I have not covered, yet. As I was conceptualizing this book, I kept coming back to the game two truths and a lie. That would become the format for this book with three myths and a legend, not necessarily true or false, but all up for discussion.

There are many people who have strong beliefs or evidence toward the validity of any of these ideas that I am calling "myths." This in no way is an authoritative or complete study of these claims. It is simply an introduction to these ideas, that will take a life of their own with further study or revelation. As we all know, these cases are constantly changing as new evidence or better forensics becomes available. However, in our "history" many things that we once believed have been changed radically when a better theory has become available. I know I am not the same person I was twenty years ago, my mindset has changed, and what I once held as the absolute truth has become open to interpretation. If you find something that really sparks your interest, I urge you to dig deeper and research it. Then share it with me so I can also expand my thinking and continue to have a fuller knowledge. So, to answer the initial question that I posed, why do we need another true crime book? We don't, but we certainly need to expand our minds and think deeply about the things that we consume. Rather than blindly listen to the great box in the corner of the room, the podcast that spouts random information from their own perspective, or the glowing rectangle we hold in our hands that gives us all kinds of misinformation. All of which I love and use but know that it is only the beginning of learning to listen to the work of others. It is from our own study that we truly gain knowledge. Welcome to the deep…

CHAPTER ONE

In the 16th century, we find an account of a woman so bloodthirsty that she still holds the record for the most prolific female murderer in the Guinness Book of World Records. She has also inspired countless authors, scriptwriters, and documentarians. As her history has become so prolific, an array of folklore, myths, and legends have cropped up, as they often do over time. There have been many authors before that have tried to separate legend from the truth, but I want to look at the legends themselves. To separate that we have to first look at the historical account and see where that leads us.

Elizabeth was born into nobility in Hungary, in 1560. Her father was Baron George VI Bathory and her mother was Baroness Anna Bathory. She had several siblings, one of her brothers served as a Judge Royal of Hungary from 1555-1605. Her family ruled over Transylvania and in 1575 her uncle, Stephen Bathory, became the King of Poland. Elizabeth was raised in the Protestant Church and would be fluent in Latin, German, Hungarian, and Greek.

The same year that her uncle became king, she was married to Ferencz Nadasdy. Their marriage would be an alliance to increase their political power and merge the lands of Transylvania and Hungary. In fact, Elizabeth never took the name of her husband because her family was more prominent and wealthier. However, in 1573, when she was thirteen years old, there was a rumor that she was pregnant by a peasant boy. The child was said to be given away to a local woman and taken to Wallachia, though the claims have never been substantiated. After their marriage, they moved from Ecsed Castle to Nadasdy Castle, although for a wedding present, Ferencz gave Elizabeth Cachtice Castle. It is reported that Ferencz loved his wife and would give her many other gifts, including building torture chambers in all of their castles and participating in the debauchery with her. In 1578, her husband became the chief commander of the Hungarian Army against the Ottomans. During that time, Elizabeth took over the business of her husband's estate at eighteen years old, where she would live in constant fear of invasion from the Ottomans.

Elizabeth would have five, or possibly six, children with her husband. The first was Anna (1585), Orsolya (1590), Katalin (1594), Andras (1596), Pal (1598), and possibly Miklos. There has also been speculation that they had several children who died in infancy and may have been lost to history. All of her children were taken care of by governesses and not by Elizabeth herself.

January 4th, 1604, her husband died at the age of forty-eight. The cause of death is unknown but he would have debilitating pain in his legs from 1601 and by 1603 he would be disabled. After his death, she moved to Cachtice Castle and the stories of murders would begin. There was talk of her killing peasants and her infamy spread into all the of the land. However, the stories weren't investigated until several noblewomen turned up dead in 1609. The investigators started collecting witness statements in 1610, and by the next year, they had over 300 statements. The accounts would include torture, by various methods, and burial locations of people she killed.

On December 30th, 1609, Elizabeth and three of her servants were arrested. Her servants were reportedly arrested as accomplices in the murders. The rumor is that they were caught in the middle of torturing a victim and covered in blood, but other accounts say they were arrested while having dinner. In the witness testimonies, many of them claimed that they heard the rumors but never saw them with their own eyes. The servants that testified did so under torture. This is one of the reasons we do not use torture as a form of obtaining testimony, as people who are being tortured will say anything. These discrepancies gave rise to the belief that there may have been no murders at all, but it may have been a way to grab the wealth of her family.

In 1611, all three of the servants would go on trial and eventually be burned alive; one was burned after being beheaded. At this time Elizabeth would then be confined to her castle. The main investigator wrote that she was locked in a bricked room, however, this seems to be a fantasy since the priests from the castle wrote that she was able to wander the castle freely. On August 20th, 1614, Elizabeth complained that her hands were cold. She would be told by the guards to lie down and rest. The next morning, they found her dead. Oddly she was not buried until November 25th, 1614, and before the villagers would force them to move the body back to her hometown and the family crypt. Her body was unmarked and today the actual location has been lost to history.

Myth #1: Elizabeth Is the Most Prolific Female Murderer of All Time

The Guinness Book of World Records counts Elizabeth as the most prolific female murderer, with over 600 victims in her body count. They claim that she killed virgins to drink their blood and bathe in it in order to preserve her youth. It is known that Elizabeth was a prolific sadist and torturer, and definitely killed some people. In her upbringing, she was taught many practices that were commonplace with the social elite. She was taught devil worship by one of her Satanist uncles and she was taught sadism by her aunt who was one of the most famous lesbians of her time. She also came from a long line of deviant family members and had the physical and mental trauma befitting familial inbreeding.

After Elizabeth was married, at the age of fifteen, every castle that she stayed in would have had a dungeon and torture chamber. She would have learned many things in her childhood and from her husband, who fought in battles with the Ottomans. Elizabeth loved to use almost any implement that she could get her hands on to cause pain to her victims. She used red hot pokers, whips, branding irons, and even her own special silver pincers that were designed to rip and tear flesh. Elizabeth was not opposed to scratching or biting. A couple of her more famous stories of torture were smearing her victims with honey and leaving them out for the bugs to devour, and placing her victims into a spiked cylindrical cage, while she prodded them with hot poker until they impaled themselves on the spikes. It is documented that she and her participants in this torture would often hurl insults or laugh and joke about the pain that they were causing.

Elizabeth would start by torturing and killing her own handmaidens, but quickly it turned into picking up strangers in the village. When she finally started to make some of the nobility disappear, they could no longer turn a blind eye. They would storm the castle to arrest her and her cohorts, but when they arrived, they would walk right into one of her famous torture sessions. She was caught red-handed. There were several of her inner circle who were tried and executed. Although Elizabeth did not have to attend the trial, they did allege over eighty counts of murder. The final count is believed to have been between 300 and 650 people that she was responsible for killing.

During this time of history, the nobles were able to get away with virtually anything given their power and influence. This makes it easy to believe that she could have gotten away with much more than the 80 counts of murder that she was charged with. However, with the passage of time, the truth can be lost, and seems to have done that in this instance. There are also those that believe that Elizabeth is completely innocent, and that the other elite only wanted to confiscate her castles and wealth. This would certainly not be the first or last time that history has shown the greed of others.

Myth #2: Elizabeth Bathed in the Blood of Virgins

The most famous story that circulates about Elizabeth Bathory is that she killed her virginal servants to bathe in their blood to preserve her youth. There are accounts of people who were drained of blood, otherwise known as exsanguination, which could point to the idea of her being a vampire or that she bathed in their blood. What history actually shows is that these instances were directly related to her torture of victims or black magic rituals. Of course, bathing in blood could certainly be part of some ritual as reported.

There was an account of a servant who was killed and the blood sprayed onto Elizabeth. It is reported that she made a comment about her skin feeling more supple where the blood had been. This was the main account that gave rise to the idea that she would do it to preserve her beauty. Although this seems plausible considering the times and her obvious penchant for the macabre, Elizabeth would die in her cell at age 54 and the bulk of her torturing and killing would happen in her late teens and twenties. This would be long before she would have even considered getting old and needing to preserve her beauty.

The most compelling argument against the idea of her bathing in blood is the fact that it is not mentioned once in any of the court documents. Those same documents go into great detail about torture, rituals, and murder but never once mention bathing in blood. These witnesses were also tortured to get the information that they gave, so how reliable is their information? There is a possibility that none of the stories are true, and all of this was politically motivated. Elizabeth Bathory may have been a victim of her time.

Over the years, we find that many of the "historical" accounts become polluted by sensational claims and the popularity of the criminals themselves. The old adage is only the winners write history. We also know that often these figures from history, without solid records, can become merged with other prolific stories of the time. It is natural for us to combine these "tall tales" that we hear about to shape our beliefs about the figures themselves. In our current culture, we see this happen in movies that are "inspired by a true story." They are often embellished and made to be much more fantastical than the real story could ever be. This often makes me wonder what people will think 1000 years from now when they discover the "true crime" movies that we watch. Will they believe that they are historical accounts, or will they know that they are fiction?

Myth #3: It Was Elizabeth's Followers Who Killed Not Her

There is a theory that it was Elizabeth's servants that actually committed the crimes and Elizabeth herself may not have been involved at all. The fact that all the servants were put to death and Elizabeth was provided house arrest seems to be the basis of this theory. They could actually prove the crimes of the servants, but they could not truly prove that Elizabeth had done anything. Elizabeth would also plead innocent to all the murders and say that it must have been the servants without her knowledge. To understand this better we need to look into who these servants were, and not only the three that were executed but also some that had been with her when the killing began.

Anna Darvulia served with the countess between 1601-1609, when she died, probably of a stroke, before the arrests happened. Although not much is known about Anna in the history books, there has been speculation that she oversaw the young female servants of Elizabeth. It was said that she was a cruel taskmaster and may have been the one who actually gave Elizabeth all the ideas to start gathering up peasant girls and torturing them. She was believed to be the countess's closest confidant and possibly the person who taught her black magic rituals and witchcraft. We will never know the extent of her involvement since she died before the trial began, but it is safe to say that Anna had a hand in everything that was done in the castle.

Janos Ujvary (Ficzko) was the youngest of Elizabeth's servants and had been with her for sixteen years at the time of the arrest. It was rumored that he was her favorite servant and would even laugh and shout insults while they tortured their victims. He admitted to knowing thirty-seven of the girls that were killed and testified to it in court. He participated in the torture, often from the sidelines, where his main responsibility was luring victims to the castle as well as disposing of their bodies afterward. He also testified that Elizabeth would participate in the torture and killings herself. At the execution, because of Ficzko's youth, they would behead him before burning his remains.

Illona Jo (Helena) was a nursemaid for Elizabeth's children and had been with her for the longest, possibly from the time of her first child with her husband. She testified to luring girls to the castle and participating in a few of the torture and killing sessions. She would not say the actual number of victims, but she detailed the crimes that were committed by everyone involved. She tells an interesting account of disposing of the blood of some of the victims, by the handful. This may be a clear indication that Elizabeth never bathed in the blood of her victims since they were disposing and hiding the blood rather than using it for another purpose. She also helped with the disposal and hiding of the bodies. She too claimed that Elizabeth helped in many of the torture and killing sessions.

Dorottya Szentes had only been at the castle for five years by the time the arrest happened. She claimed to have been lured to the castle by Helena and agreed to participate so she would not become one of the victims. She testified to thirty-six tortures and killings, but because of her short time with the countess may not have known about the many others before her arrival. She would also admit to luring victims, torturing, murdering, and burying them.

Katalin Benenczky was with the countess for ten years as a washerwoman. She was the only servant who did not want to participate in the torture. All the other servants would say that she was the least cruel of the lot. They would have to force her to participate in the torture and it is claimed that she would sneak food and water to the victims. She was even caught and disciplined herself. She testified to fifty killings as well as hiding and burying the victims that were tortured by everyone else. She was the only servant that was not executed with the rest and sentenced to life imprisonment.

So, is it true that Anna, Ficzko, and Helena were the three that spearheaded the torture, murder, and rituals at the castle, like Elizabeth would report? It is unlikely that the lady of the house would not know exactly what was happening in her own castle. It is interesting that her own husband was a likely participant before his death. It is certain that he would have built the torture chambers for Elizabeth and her servants to use later for these exact purposes. I do not believe that Elizabeth was innocent of the crimes that she was accused of, but I am certain that they all had their hand in the bloodlust that happened in that castle.

Legend: Elizabeth was a Vampire

The original Dracula story comes from the exploits of another Romanian from the same area, whom we affectionately call Vlad the Impaler. Vlad Tepes was the son of Vlad Dracul and the warrior leader of Wallachia. He was known for impaling victims and being a ruthless warrior on the battlefield. Consequently, that is where he died in 1477. The stories of Vlad's exploits would have been legendary by the time Elizabeth was born in 1560. The fact that she would end up being nicknamed Lady Dracula was very fitting.

The vampire lore may have started with Vlad but the mythology around vampires has only increased and evolved over the years. Our idea of vampires is very different than the idea of vampires during Elizabeth's day. Even the term "vampyr" did not appear until 18th century poetry (1748) by Heinrich Ossenfelder. The first story believed to be written about a vampire was by John Polidori called "The Vampyre" in 1819. Bram Stoker's *Dracula* did not appear until 1897 but would revolutionize our modern idea of what the vampire is.

The idea of a "vampire", roughly translated from the Slavic "upior" to mean "ghost monster", during Elizabeth Bathory's lifetime more closely resembled a poltergeist than what we currently picture as a vampire. Their idea of this being was not a physical creature but a spirit that did not drink blood and could not create more by biting them. They were rather spreaders of disease and were often blamed for plagues (or the Plague) and other communicable diseases of the day. These were the local ideas of the Slavic countries in the 1600s but would soon spread to the rest of Europe, just after Elizabeth's death in the 1700s, and gain many new qualities.

The thought that Elizabeth Bathory could be a vampire is obviously not possible because the idea of that creature did not even come into creation until after her death, but the fact that her life may have furthered the inspiration of such creatures is entirely possible. The fact that she tortured her victims and enjoyed biting them until they bled is a direct relation to the idea of vampires that we have today.

Another fact of her life that may have influenced the vampire mythology, is that she was prone to fainting seizures and severe headaches. She was most certainly epileptic, which they called fainting sickness at the time. During her time there were few treatments for such an ailment. This was before they even understood that epilepsy was a brain disorder. There were many people in her family that believed that she was possessed by a demon. They would often treat the condition with herbal remedies or exorcism, though one of the most popular medical treatments of the day was bloodletting, which was used to treat a host of conditions. This treatment could have fed ideas to Elizabeth, leading to a fondness for blood, and give rise to the idea that she needed blood to survive.

Expand Your Mind

Podcasts
- *Murder Metal Mayhem* - Ep. 221 – "Elizabeth Bathory: The Blood Countess"
- *TimeSuck w/ Dan Cummins* - Ep. 46 – "Blood Countess Elizabeth Bathory"
- *Last Podcast on the Left* - Ep. 81 – "Female Serial Killers"
- *Killer Psyche* – "Elizabeth Bathory: The Blood Countess"

Books
- *Blood Countess* by Lana Popovic
- *Bathory: Memoir of a Countess* by A. Mordeaux
- *Countess Elizabeth Bathory* by Charles River Editors

Documentaries
- *Serial Killer Culture TV* (2017) Season 2 Ep. 4 – "Infamous Bathory" - by John Borowski

CHAPTER TWO

JACK THE RIPPER

For many people, the five plus murders that occurred in Whitechapel in 1888 really cemented their interest in true crime. Jack the Ripper may be the world's most infamous serial killer and true crime case. No other case has had more investigation, more books written about the case, and more impact on pop culture than the case of Jack the Ripper. There are Ripperologists out there who only study this case. I was hooked on the Jack the Ripper case after watching the movie *From Hell* starring Johnny Depp as Inspector Abbeline. In this case there have been over one hundred suspects with no real leads, running the gamut from an American actor to a member of royalty. The truth is the case is so old we will never really know who the culprit was. However, it is still so much fun to debate about who the killer could be.

If you believe the common story of the Jack the Ripper case, there are only five murders. All five of the women were prostitutes in the Whitechapel area of London. Mary Nichols, Annie Chapman, Elizabeth Stride, Catherine Eddowes, and Mary Kelly are the five confirmed victims of the killer that was named Jack the Ripper. During the time of the killings, the killer also sent letters to the police taunting them as well as sending parts of his victims to prove that he had, in fact, committed the crimes.

On August 31st, 1888, the first victim, Mary Nichols, was found in Buck's Row. She had bruising around her jawline, which suggests that she was beaten or choked before her throat was slashed. After she was deceased, there were postmortem slashes on her abdomen and stab wounds to her genitals. When we look at this murder, in context with the other four murders, it seems that this was only the beginning of his carnage, although there has always been the possibility of murders attributed to Jack the Ripper before this crime.

The second victim, Annie Chapman, was found on September 8th. She was found less than half a mile from the first victim. This victim was also strangled before her throat was slit. As we will find out through the ages, often the killers will progress in their fantasy, and we see a refining of their craft. In the case of Annie Chapman, he would disembowel her. He took her intestines and draped them over one of her shoulders and then removed parts of her bladder, vagina, uterus, and ovaries. This would give rise to the idea that Jack the Ripper must have had some anatomical knowledge, was he a butcher or even a doctor?

On September 25th the first letter was written and mailed a few days later. This is the infamous "Dear Boss" letter. It is also the letter that is signed "Jack the Ripper" and how we arrived at the name of this elusive killer. In the letter, he mocks the police and laughs about killing prostitutes, and mentions that he isn't even close to being done. He gives some insight showing that he may have some inside information since he knows details about the possible suspects and theories on his identity.

The next two victims were savagely killed in the early morning of September 30th. Elizabeth Stride was the first victim found around 1:00 a.m. just off Berner Street. Only her throat was slashed with no other mutilation. This gave rise to the theory that he must have been interrupted and was not able to finish the job. This must have infuriated him and just forty-five minutes later another body was found in Mitre Square. This was the body of Catherine Eddowes. She was slashed across the face, her throat cut, and she was also disemboweled with her intestines placed all around her neck. Most notably, her kidney was removed, and she had a superficial wound beneath her ear. In his first letter, he would mention taking his next victim's ear and mailing it to the police. Instead, he would do that with her kidney. He would also take the time to scrawl a message on the wall stating, "The Juwes are the men that will not be blamed for nothing." This led to speculation that Jack the Ripper may have disliked the Jewish people and have been trying to cause a riot against the Jewish community. During this time, the police were calling the criminal "Leather Apron" and believed that he was Jewish.

The final canonical murder was reported on November 9th, when the grisly scene of Mary Kelly would be found. This was the only murder that was found indoors, and he would use that to really take his time. Mary Kelly was found with her throat cut so deeply she was almost decapitated. He would skin her forehead and remove both her nose and ears. He sliced both her legs from ankle to knee and nearly severed her left arm at the shoulder. She was also disemboweled with her liver draped across one of her legs. He severed her breasts and laid them on the nightstand with her kidneys, heart, and nose. The walls were covered in blood and strips of flesh. Mary was also found to be three months pregnant, but both the uterus and fetus were taken by the killer.

Strangely, this would be the final canonical murder that was attributed to this killer. This serial killer that has stood the test of time and fascinated several generations of people, would only be actively killing for three months. The murders started suddenly and then ended just as abruptly. There have been countless researchers that have pored over all the information for over one hundred years and still come up fruitless. This has given rise to some wild theories about the case. Did the murders stop? Was the killer imprisoned or die? Or did he finally achieve his goal and no longer needed to kill? I don't believe that a killer such as this, could stop. I believe he either moved on and continued to kill or he may have died. As we see the continual ramping up in frenzy throughout all five of the canonical killings, the killer would have been unable to stop his insatiable desire to do it again.

Myth #1: Jack the Ripper Only Killed Prostitutes

When we discuss the victims of Jack the Ripper, we need to take a hard look at his hunting grounds. During the time of Jack the Ripper, London was starkly divided. The West End, where all the aristocrats and wealthy lived was very posh. On the other hand, the East End was the worst of the worst and was populated by the extremely poor. With that came thieves, gangs, crime, and disease. Whitechapel was the very heart of the East End of London. It was a dark place where every imaginable crime was going on. In terms of today, it would be the place where the police barely even respond. The number of people who were starving and living on the street was immense. This was a buffet table for the most infamous serial killer of all time.

When we take a hard look at the five women thought to be the only victims of Jack the Ripper, we find out some surprising things. The first thing is that none of them were actually from Whitechapel. They all have their own stories, which you should definitely look into. The truth is no matter what the reason all five of them ended up in Whitechapel and were taken into the depths from which they would never return.

We have been told so many times that "Saucy" Jack only killed prostitutes, that it has become fact. In reality, only two of Jack's five victims can reliably traced to sex work and only one was a current practicing prostitute on the night of her murder. Mary Jane Kelly was working the night Jack the Ripper would strike and Elizabeth Stride was a former sex worker. The other three women Mary Nichols, Annie Chapman, and Catherine Eddowes were all hard-working women with jobs as servants.

Mary Nichols was married with five children, though she was separated from her husband and children, because of his cheating and her drinking. She would become a prolific drunk and end up moving around London often staying at the Lambeth Workhouse, finally ending up in the East End. While there, she would often end up spending all her lodging money on alcohol and sleeping on the street, which was a common practice for the day. On the night she was murdered, this is exactly what happened, and sadly, she would meet Jack.

Annie Chapman would work on the street selling crochet work and artificial flowers to passersby. She would also supplement that income with prostitution, but she was no means a full-time sex worker. The night before she was killed, she would end up suffering a beating from someone, though it is unknown who she got into a scuffle with. On that final day, she would be short on lodging money and go out to make some quick money doing sex work; sadly, that would be her last day on earth.

There isn't much known about Catherine Eddowes other than she had many different jobs through the years and before ending up in the East End. She was known to be a bit of a drunk with a feisty temper. On the night that she was killed, she would be the second victim of Jack, and she had just been released from jail after being arrested for public drunkenness.

The popularized idea that Jack would solicit these women for sex, take them to a secluded location, and kill them is almost completely false. Upon reviewing the medical reports, most of the victims were killed while reclining and possibly sleeping. It was common practice, during this time, that if you couldn't pay for lodging you would find a place to sleep on the street. All four women that were found outside were in their forties and had lived difficult lives. Three of those women regularly slept on the street and showed no signs of struggle when their bodies were found. This begs another question, if the truth is that Jack the Ripper primarily killed sleeping women, why did the media paint him as a vicious sexual killer of prostitutes? Could it be that their news media was not that different from our own? We live in a moment of time where the media often creates headlines to have a "story", shaping our thought patterns and spoon-feeding us the "truth". Never in our history has the "truth" been more available to us, all to create what "they" want us to believe. We can see that sensationalism playing out in the time of Jack the Ripper as well. It certainly makes for a better headline when Jack is killing unsavory ladies, rather than innocent sleeping women. We should also remember that unlike in our time of the internet, cell phones, and constant news reporting, they only had the papers and word of mouth to get their "news".

Myth #2: Jack the Ripper Looked Like an Aristocrat

I always find it interesting that when we imagine Jack the Ripper, we always picture him as a figure just on the edge of the shadows, immaculately dressed, covered in a black cloak, and adorned with a black top hat. The idea that this wouldn't have stood out like a sore thumb in the East End of London at that time is ridiculous. Most people in London in the East End were hardworking people, like dock workers, and would have dressed as such. The eyewitness accounts do say that the man was wearing a long dark jacket and a felt hat; however, the idea that he was dressed like he was about to go to the opera is false. His clothing would have been a little worn, possibly tattered. If not, they would have been able to identify this killer in record fashion.

Since there are, literally, hundreds of suspects in this case I cannot cover them all, but we should definitely touch on a few of them. The seven suspects that we will look at more closely in the Jack the Ripper case are Aaron Kosminski, Prince Albert Victor, Dr. Thomas Neill Cream, Severin Klosovksi, Francis Tumblety, Montague John Druitt, and Walter Sickert.

Aaron Kosminski
- A Polish Jewish man, who lived close to the site of the murders. He was also a barber. In 1891, he was committed to an asylum because he threatened his sister

with a knife. While in the asylum he seemed to be a model patient, but he would ultimately pass away in 1919.

- The reason why people believe that he could be Jack the Ripper begins with the investigators themselves. They would mention a suspect named "Kosminski" and that he was placed in an asylum. Of course, this could be one of many with the last name, but the fact that Aaron was thought to hate women and was good with a knife, turned the spotlight on him.

- In 2014, Russell Edwards named Aaron Kosminski as Jack the Ripper in his book *Naming Jack the Ripper*. He cites a DNA study that was performed on a shawl that was found with the body of Catherine Eddowes. The shawl had mitochondrial DNA that matched both Eddowes and Kosminski. This study has been widely criticized by academics since it was published.

- The biggest mark against Kosminski is the fact that he was placed in the asylum in 1891 but the canonical murders ended in 1888. Of course, this is only a problem if you believe there are only five murders.

Prince Albert Victor

- The most famous of the Ripper suspects. He has given rise to the conspiracy about the Royals committing the murders. Although he may have been mildly low functioning or have had syphilis, during the time of the murders he was never a suspect. In fact, the theories about Prince Albert Victor would not begin until 1962 when he was first mentioned as a suspect.

- The Royal Family Conspiracy Theory first reared its head in 1973 but wasn't really fleshed out until Stephen Knight's book *Jack the Ripper: The Final Solution* in 1978. In Knight's theory, Prince Albert Victor was introduced to Annie Crook by Walter Sickert. He would get her pregnant and she would give birth to a baby girl they named Alice. However, when the Queen discovered the scandal, she ordered the child terminated. Prince Albert Victor and Annie Crook would be taken away and institutionalized, and the child would escape with the nanny, Mary Kelly. Alice would be taken to a convent and Mary Kelly would tell all of her friends about the scandal. They would then attempt to blackmail the monarchy.

- The monarchy would decide to kill all of the women involved, using masonic rites to accomplish this. They would use Jack the Ripper as a symbol and help engage the cover up. Ultimately, they would kill Montague John Druitt, making it look like a suicide, to pin the murders on. Alice would grow up and eventually marry Walter Sickert, another suspect of the Ripper murders.

- This fanciful story has been debunked by many Ripperologists, although there are still many people who hold this as their conclusion. The truth is there is little evidence to tie Prince Albert Victor to the Jack the Ripper murders. In fact, there is evidence that he was not even in London during the majority of the murders.

Dr. Thomas Neill Cream

- A medical doctor and a serial killer (aside from being a suspect in the Jack the Ripper murders). He would poison his victims with strychnine and murder up to ten people in three countries (Canada, United States, and England). He would eventually be hanged in 1892.

- It is without a doubt that Dr. Thomas killed prostitutes and women who were less fortunate. However, his method of killing is vastly different from the Jack the Ripper victims. Jack the Ripper eviscerated his victims while Dr. Thomas preferred poisoning them. The most glaring flaw in this theory is the fact that Dr. Thomas didn't return to London until 1891. He was in prison in Illinois from 1881 to 1891 for the poisoning death of Daniel Stott. There is no way that he could be Jack the Ripper.

Severin Klosovski (aka George Chapman)

- A nurse and doctor's assistant who lived in Poland until 1886 or 1887. He moved to the East End of London in late 1887 or 1888 becoming a barber assistant. He would eventually open his own barbershop at 126 Cable Street and marry a Polish girl in 1889, even though he was already married in Poland. In 1891, they moved to Jersey City, NJ and had many problems culminating with his attempt to kill her. They would both move back to London by 1893.

- In 1893, he met a woman named Annie Chapman (no relation to the Ripper victim) and he changed his name to George Chapman. He would end up taking four mistresses and kill three of them by poisoning, making him a verified serial killer. He killed Mary Isabella Spink in 1897, Bessie Taylor in 1901, and Maud Marsh in 1902. There is no clear motive for the murders since he received little to no money for any of them.

- Chapman did arrive in Whitechapel right around the time of the first canonical Jack the Ripper murder and lived there throughout the course of the five murders. He was never a named suspect during the initial investigation however, the main investigator Frederick Abberline was reported to say that they had finally caught Jack the Ripper when Chapman was arrested. Other than those two things there is little physical evidence to connect Chapman to any of the crimes. He was a well-known misogynist and eventual killer, but does that make him Jack the Ripper? If so, why would he change his method of murder? Jack the Ripper slit the throat and eviscerated his victims, but Chapman preferred to poison his victims.

Dr. Francis Tumblety

- Born in Ireland, he was a well-known medical quack, who posed as the "Indian Herb" doctor throughout North America. He would travel all over the world meeting people and swindling them out of money and selling them his "cure-all" medicines.
- In 1875, Tumblety fled Liverpool after someone died from ingesting his medication. He would then move to London and eventually be arrested for indecency on November 7th, 1888 (two days before the body of Mary Kelly was found). Scotland Yard would become increasingly interested in him for the recent murders, but on November 20th he fled to France and on November 24th he returned to the United States. He passed away from heart disease on May 28th, 1903.
- Although there is little physical evidence to connect Tumblety to the Jack the Ripper murders, he was there during the murders and fled just after the canonical murders ended. If you believe there were only five Jack the Ripper murders, Tumblety is a strong candidate. It is also well known that he had a failed relationship with a prostitute, which gave him a hatred of women, specifically prostitutes. The Ripperologists often cite that Tumblety was shorter than the eyewitness reports and none of them mentioned Tumblety's prominent mustache. Of course, it was dark, and he may have trimmed the mustache so he wouldn't be easily identified.

Montague John Druitt

- A native, born in Wimborne Minster, Dorset, England, who grew up in an upper-middle-class family. He was educated, eventually becoming a school teacher, and had a small law practice. Druitt was also very active in sports and was an avid Cricket player. In November 1888, for unknown reasons, he lost his job as a teacher and the following month he was found drowned in the Thames River.

- Although much of the evidence against Druitt is circumstantial, the odd timing of his apparent "suicide" makes him a suspect. The finger would be pointed at him because his death would also signal the end of the murders. As soon as the Mary Kelly murder happened there were rumors about the Ripper drowning in the River Thames. This was officially stated in 1891 in a session of Parliament. It is said that even the Druitt family believed that he was Jack the Ripper.

- It has been proven that on several days when the murders occurred, Druitt was either playing cricket or in a courtroom. There could still be ample time for him to travel into Whitechapel, commit the murders, and get home. However, could he make it back home covered in blood and go unnoticed by anyone else? Even the leading investigator, Frederick Abberline, did not believe that Druitt had anything to do with the murders.

Walter Sickert

- Walter was an eccentric British painter, who took a keen interest in the Jack the Ripper case. He would stay in one of the rooms believed to be used by the killer and even paint artwork that was inspired by the crimes. He was never mentioned until the 1970s when he was thought to be an accomplice of Jack the Ripper. The graphic novel, and later movie, *From Hell* was based on the theory that was outlined in the 1976 book Jack the Ripper: The Final Solution.

- In 2002, Patricia Cornwell released a book, *Portrait of a Killer: Jack the Ripper-Case Closed*. In this book, she officially names Sickert as the killer. She would maintain that mitochondrial DNA from one of the Ripper letters could have only been traced to Walter Sickert. There was also a rumor that she destroyed one of Sickert's paintings to get more DNA to connect him to the Ripper case. She has since denied these claims.
- There is very little other evidence to suggest that Sickert was anything more than obsessed with the biggest story of his time. He really would have fit right in with our culture that has taken such an interest in true crime.

There is so much debate on who Jack the Ripper is; the only thing that we can be certain about is that a person named Jack the Ripper killed. We have zero knowledge of the real name of the killer. Not only that, but we are not even sure if the killer was male or female. The name Jack the Ripper, that has stuck for eternity, is as much myth and legend as the murders themselves.

Myth #3: Jack the Ripper Only Killed 5 Victims

We have discussed the five canonical victims of Jack the Ripper, starting with Mary Nichols and ending with Mary Kelly. However, is that the real final number? We have already ascertained that the media frenzy around the case distorted many facts, as did the passage of time and new "evidence" that has been injected into the case. The original police files and press reports show no evidence of the idea of a "canonical five". In fact, that term is not even mentioned until 1987 by Martin Fido.

In the original Whitechapel Murders case file, there were actually eleven named victims of Jack the Ripper, but there is the possibility that there were at least twelve or even more. There were two before the murder of Mary Nichols and five after the murder of Mary Kelly. The first attack was in the early hours of April 3rd, 1888, when Emma Smith was attacked by an unknown group of people. Emma initially survived the attack but was wounded severely. She made it back to the lodging house and they would convince her to go to the hospital, where she would die the following day. Before she passed, she told the doctor that she was attacked by a group of men. This would be the main reason people discounted it as the first Ripper victim.

The second murder was on August 7th, 1888, when the body of Martha Tabram was found. She was definitely a prostitute, who was taken to a dark alley by a potential client and murdered. She had been stabbed 39 times from the throat to the abdomen. The investigating doctor said that he believed that two different blades were used. The majority of the wounds were done by a small knife but the final death blow, to the sternum, was with a bayonet or long knife. The body was also placed in a similar fashion to the five canonical victims. One thing to note: the investigators of the time believed this to be one of the Ripper's victims. There is a real possibility that this was part of his growth into his modus operandi.

The first victim after the Mary Kelly murder was Rose Mylett. She was seen with two sailors at 2:30 a.m. on December 20th, 1888, and she seemed to be very drunk. Her body would be found at 4:30 a.m. and the police initially believed it to be a suicide or a sudden death. However, the postmortem report would find that Rose was strangled to death with a wire from behind. The police, believing that it was accidental, would not investigate it as a murder. The media then immediately associated the murder with Jack the Ripper. Although the method of killing would be strangulation, it was postulated that the Ripper may have strangled all the victims and then hidden the fact by cutting their throats. Could this be another victim of Jack the Ripper? Most people believe that Rose was not, but she is named in the official report.

Another six months would pass and on July 17th, 1889, Alice Mackenzie was found murdered. Alice was about forty-five years old, a local prostitute, and was found at 12:50 a.m. lying close to a lamp post. Her body was found with her skirt pulled up and a superficial wound from her left breast down to her navel. The majority of the investigators did not believe that this was the work of Jack the Ripper, even though the media was clamoring for it.

On September 10th, 1889, an unknown woman was found on Pinchin Street at 5:20 a.m. the body was found by a police officer and believed to have been placed there sometime after his 5:00 a.m. check of the area. There was no blood in the area, so the body must have been murdered elsewhere. The body was determined to have been killed thirty-six hours prior. This would mean that the victim would be killed on the anniversary of the Annie Chapman murder. There was no mutilation of the body, but complete dismemberment. The torso that was found was never identified and is widely considered to not be the work of Jack the Ripper. The differences in the modus operandi between the Ripper and this murderer are almost too much to overcome.

The final victim thought to be a possible murder of Jack the Ripper was Frances Coles. Her body was found at 2:15 a.m. on February 13th, 1891, by Constable Ernest Thompson. The constable had passed the spot at 2:00 a.m. and there had been no body. When he found the body, it was lying in a pool of blood with her throat slashed from ear to ear. When they finally identified the woman, a suspect would come to light, Thomas Saddler. He knew the victim and she was a witness to him being robbed the night of the murder. He blamed her for not intervening in the robbery. He was arrested and charged with the murder of Frances Coles, but ultimately released for lack of evidence.

The mystery remains, did Jack the Ripper kill only five victims, or did he murder many more? Did he move to another location and begin killing there? Did he die, or was he arrested for something else? In over 146 years we have not been able to come to a clear conclusion on this case, but it will remain ever fascinating for those that choose to dig in.

Legend: Jack the Ripper Was a Woman

In the 1959 book, *The Identity of Jack the Ripper*, the author Donald McCormick notes that Inspector Abberline himself held the possibility that the killer might be a woman. This theory would be around from just after the final canonical murder of Mary Kelly. It is interesting to me that after seeing the brutality of all the other four murders attributed to Jack the Ripper Abberline would come up with the theory that Jack might actually be a Jill. As he was tossing around ideas about the murders with his mentor Dr. Thomas Dutton, Jill the Ripper would become a central theme.

This theory would come about because of testimony given by Caroline Maxwell, who was a resident of the area. The investigators estimated the time of death of Mary Kelly to be between 3:30 and 4:00 a.m. on November 9th, 1888. All of the forensics of the day would also support that hypothesis. Caroline Maxwell would testify to having seen Mary Kelly twice, several hours after the medical examiners believed her to be deceased. The first time was between 8:00 and 8:30 a.m. and she said that she looked very sick. She then saw her again talking to a man outside the Britannia Public House just an hour later.

The fact that Caroline was a trustworthy witness and had never faltered from her descriptions and times, gave Abberline pause to question his current idea of who the murderer could be. His theory was that the killer may have dressed in Mary Kelly's clothing to disguise herself and that was who Caroline saw the day of the murder. To his credit,

Dr. Dutton thought it was a stretch but said that if it was a woman it would have to be a midwife. This is where the initial theory goes from Jill the Ripper to the "mad midwife" theory.

There are a few points of the theory that could be plausible. The first point that has some weight is the fact that all of Whitechapel was looking for a man, Jack the Ripper, which would allow for a woman to go undiscovered. A woman would be able to get close to another woman, especially when every woman was on high alert for a killer on the loose. The other points all lead to reasons why a midwife specifically would be the perfect choice. Midwives would be seen at all hours in the Whitechapel district, so it would not be uncommon nor out of place. A midwife's clothing often was covered in blood and would be discarded after medical procedures. Again, it would not be uncommon to see. They were already looking for a barber, butcher, or physician for the murders. The next person who would have the anatomical knowledge needed to eviscerate the victims would be a midwife.

The first person to write about the theory of Jill the Ripper was William Stewart in his 1939 book, *Jack the Ripper: A New Theory*. He would state all the other reasons, but he would focus on the practice where midwives would use pressure points to render their patients unconscious. Stewart would also theorize that Mary Kelly was actually having a routine abortion when the "mad midwife" struck.

This theory, while having some plausible notes, is considered to have a low probability of truth. What is much more likely is that Jack the Ripper would dress up in women's clothing to gain the trust of his victims or to attempt an escape and avoid detection. This would be a theory that was held by Sir Arthur Conan Doyle. But of course, he was also a huge proponent for Spiritualists, who were proven to be frauds by Harry Houdini.

Expand Your Mind

Podcasts
- *TimeSuck w/ Dan Cummins* - Bonus Ep. 21 – "Jack the Ripper!"
- *Last Podcast on the Left* - Eps. 254-258 – "Jack the Ripper"
- *Killer Psyche* – "Jack the Ripper"

Books
- *The Ultimate Jack the Ripper Sourcebook* by Stewart Evans & Keith Skinner
- *Jack the Ripper: The Complete Casebook* by Donald Rumbelow

Documentaries & Movies
- *Jack the Ripper: London's Most Notorious Killer* (2020)
- *Jack the Ripper: The Case Reopened* (2019)
- *Jack the Ripper: The Definitive Story* (2011)
- *From Hell* (2001) by Hughes Brothers

CHAPTER THREE

HERMAN W. MUDGETT

Many of you may not even know this prolific serial killer by name. Over the years he would take on many names, but Herman Webster Mudgett was his birth name. The infamous name that we know him by is Dr. Henry Howard Holmes or more affectionately H.H. Holmes. Holmes is a fascinating figure shrouded in mystery and along with that come all the myths and legends. My favorite documentarian, author, and friend, John Borowski, has done the preeminent story of the life of H.H. Holmes in his documentary *H.H. Holmes: America's First Serial Killer*.

Holmes lived at the turn of the century, commonly believed to be born in 1861, and was active just before the turn of the century. This time period in our history gave rise to the circus sideshow and P.T. Barnum. The showman and the swindler were part of the American culture of the day. Holmes would eventually become part of this lore of American history. He was living in Chicago during the 1893 World's Columbian Exposition (World's Fair) and, if believed, committed the majority of his murders during that time. Holmes was also a prolific criminal who was always interested in swindling someone to further his monetary gain. He was famous for being a con artist and even married several women just to get their money.

Holmes grew up in Gilmanton, New Hampshire, attended Phillips Exeter Academy for grade school, and Gilmanton Academy where he graduated high school with honors at sixteen years old. His parents were church going Methodists, owned a farm, and worked in several different businesses. His father was a drunk that often treated his family badly. Holmes would also struggle with bullying in school because of his exceptional academics. Later in life, Holmes' would recount a formative moment with his bullies. The other boys forced young Herman into a doctor's office to scare him with the skeleton that hung there. This would be the first moment that Holmes would be face to face with death. They pushed Herman into the skeleton, and although he was frightened at first, he would come to realize that it truly excited him. He would count this event as the catalyst for his obsession with death.

In 1882, Holmes attended the University of Michigan in the Department of Medicine and Surgery. He would graduate only two years later. It was during this time period that Holmes, along with his professor William Herdman, would begin grave robbing and selling the cadavers for medical use. Holmes would later admit to committing insurance fraud by using these cadavers, while he was in college. This is the same scheme that he would use later in life, by attempting to fake his own death. He would take out an insurance policy on a person and use one the cadavers to "prove" that the person was dead, therefore fooling the insurance company to pay out the policy, with him being the sole beneficiary.

Holmes moved to Chicago in 1886 and just a year later would start the building project for which he would become infamous: the "hotel", that would become known as "The Murder Castle". He started construction in 1887, initially planning to build a two-story building with retail spaces on the first floor and apartments on the second floor. He was sued by his first construction company in 1888 for non-payment. As construction was underway in 1892, he added a third floor saying that he would use it for hotel space for the World's Columbian Exposition. There are lots of claims about the "Murder Castle" including hidden passageways, doors that go nowhere, gas chambers, chutes to the basement, etc. What is truly known is that Holmes hired and fired many builders in the construction of the "Murder Castle".

The common belief is that Holmes built the "Murder Castle" to lure in tourists who were visiting the World's Exposition so he could kill them and sell their cadavers to medical schools. It has been proven that he did sell cadavers during college, but he didn't kill anyone during that time. Although there have been many claims about the events at the "Murder Castle" none of them have ever been proven. Shortly after his arrest the "Murder Castle" would be burnt to the ground by an unknown arsonist.

For all the mythology that has arisen around this case, Holmes was only convicted of one murder: his business partner and accomplice Benjamin Pitezel in 1894. The two had concocted a scheme of fraud against the insurance company. They would take out a $10,000 life insurance policy on Pietzel and fake his death. Pietzel would play an inventor named, "B.F. Perry" and be killed and disfigured in a lab explosion. Only instead of faking the death Holmes chloroformed him and then burned the body. Holmes then tried to procure a cadaver to pose as Pietzel for the "accident". At the trial, it was proven that Pietzel was dead before the chloroform was used, which now made the crime murder. Holmes was convicted and hanged on November 17th, 1894. It still begs the question; did Holmes really intend to kill Pietzel or was it just a scheme gone wrong?

Myth #1: The "Murder Castle" Was a Hotel of Horrors

Holmes was very secretive about his plans for the "Murder Castle." He had many different crews working on the building and would only tell them what they needed to build that day. He would then fire them and not pay them for their work, before bringing in another crew to work on a different part of the building. This brought rise to all kinds of speculation about the building itself.

The first floor was a functioning retail space and had several businesses that operated there. It was the top two floors that took a significant time to build. It is said that the second floor had six hallways and fifty doors. There were thirty-five rooms that could be used as bedrooms. There were soundproofed rooms, rooms lined in asbestos (thought to be used to burn people alive), rooms that had gas pipes run into them, hidden peepholes, alarms (in case of an escape), trapdoors, secret passageways, and a chute that led to the basement. The third floor was reported to be very erratic. The rooms were built at odd angles and often had no room numbers. There were dead ends and staircases that led nowhere. The basement was said to include an extensive torture chamber, vats of acid, autopsy tables, and a crematorium.

There are reports of what awaited the police as they began investigating the "Murder Castle" after Holmes' arrest in 1894. There has been more recent speculation that all of this was fabricated by the news media of the day. What was reportedly found was largely in the basement. There was an autopsy table that was covered in blood. They found an array of medical tools, acids, women's clothing, and bones. The bones that they found were largely animal bones but also some human. After some research, they were determined to be from a young child, about 7 or 8 years old. It was believed that Holmes was still in the business of dissecting bodies, selling their bones to medical institutions, and selling their organs. It became well known that Holmes was a grave robber, and it was thought that he used the "Murder Castle" to obtain fresher victims and continue the lucrative business that he had created.

Sadly, we may never know the full truth about the "Murder Castle". Holmes was arrested on November 17th, 1894, for the murder of Benjamin Pietzel. The "Murder Castle" would be sold and there were plans to turn it into a museum for Holmes' crimes, but shortly after his arrest, the top two floors burned down. Was this an attempt by Holmes' accomplices to cover up the truth about his crimes? Or was this an attempt to get rid of any evidence so Holmes would be able to get out of jail? The truth was hidden in the flames and the inextinguishable speculation about the infamous H.H. Holmes would rise from its ashes.

Myth #2: Holmes Killed More Than 200 People

The belief that Holmes killed over 200 people comes from the inflated news reports around the "Murder Castle" and the World's Colombian Exposition. The news media would take the claims of missing people and immediately attribute those to deaths within the "Murder Castle." However, with minimal forensics, they have never been able to determine who the bodies were in the basement. They certainly could have been attendees of the "Murder Castle", or they may have been stolen bodies. We will simply never know the true body count of Holmes. In his first confession, he admitted to several crimes including fraud and swindling, but denied any murder. However, the second confession is where Holmes would claim twenty-seven murders, including his wives, business partners, and other people. Ultimately, they would be able to conclusively prove fourteen murders that Holmes had committed. There were several people that he claimed to have killed that were found alive and well.

Holmes would only be convicted of the murder of Benjamin Pitezel and was sentenced to death. After the life insurance scam and murder, he planned to kidnap Benjamin's wife Carrie and his three children. He needed Carrie to identify Benjamin's body so he could collect the insurance money, but Carrie sent her fourteen-year-old daughter to identify the body. Oddly, Holmes would let Carrie Pitezel live, but the three children would not be so lucky. He sent Carrie away on a train and took the three children. On October 10th, 1894, the son Howard disappeared. Holmes had purchased some drugs from the pharmacy that he would use to kill the young boy. Then on October 25th, he would place both girls in a trunk that he drilled a hole in and connected a hose and fill the trunk with gas, asphyxiating the girls. In total we know that Holmes killed at least four people, all members of the Pitezel family.

Holmes was presumed to have murdered several others including his mistress Julia Smythe and her daughter Pearl Conner. They both disappeared on Christmas Eve, 1891. Holmes would claim that she left to visit her dying sister, then said she went back to her husband, before finally he would say she died during an abortion. He confessed to poisoning Pearl and when they excavated his cellar they would find a skeleton of a child about her age. His secretary Emeline Cigrand was last seen in December of 1892. Her family was informed that she left to marry a "Robert Phelps." The police believed that she had been pregnant by Holmes and also died in a botched abortion. Her skeleton was found in the possession of another physician who articulated skeletons for Holmes. He was also presumed to have killed a twenty-four-year-old actress and her eighteen-year-old sister, Wilhelmina and Nannie Williams. Holmes would get Wilhelmina to sign over property to him using one of his many aliases. On July 5th, 1893, Nannie wrote to her aunt saying that she was going to Europe with Harry and sis, and that they need not worry about her anymore. The two sisters would never be heard from again.

There would be at least eleven other disappearances or murders that Holmes was suspected of committing, but they did not have any conclusive evidence. This is definitely more than the original Pitezel murders but a far cry from the hundreds of victims that Holmes is believed to have killed. The real body count has been lost to time and history.

Myth #3: Holmes Was Jack the Ripper

This has become a pretty recent theory that has been popularized by Holmes' great-great-grandson, Jeff Mudgett. He would write a book called *Bloodstains*, which is his own research into two diaries that were handed down to him from his great-great-grandfather. In this book, he postulates that Holmes was in London with an assistant of his during the Jack the Ripper murders. Apparently, Holmes had been diagnosed with a brain tumor and believed he needed to harvest body parts to extend his life. He would then instruct his assistant on how to kill and harvest the necessary parts that he would need. So, this begs the question, is it Holmes that was Jack the Ripper or the assistant? Another interesting aspect of this theory is that Holmes would be diagnosed with a brain tumor in or before 1888. The first successful documentation of a complete removal of a brain tumor was early in 1887, by Robert F. Weir and the patient would die shortly after. The idea that Holmes would have been diagnosed of this relatively "new" phenomenon, with the first reported case in 1881, and that he would choose to travel to London to procure his victims, seems a little far-fetched. It wouldn't be until 1895, after Holmes was arrested, that the x-ray was even discovered. Why wouldn't he stay in Chicago to kill his victims, especially if he was sick? There is no indication that Holmes was sick during this time, in fact, many of his schemes would happen after 1888.

It is a clever theory because it avoids the most common objection, that the methods of killing, between Holmes and Jack the Ripper, are completely different. Jack the Ripper was a frenzy killer, who seemed to kill because he took exception to ladies who lived on the street in the Whitechapel area. He used a knife and seemed to be enraged at several of the murder scenes. On the other hand, Holmes seemed to be a very calculated killer. He gassed people and did not prefer to use a knife until after death, where he would dismember the bodies for disposal or sale. This is still the most compelling argument against Holmes being Jack the Ripper. Although, we often see a serial killer refine their method of murder, we almost never see a killer completely change their style of killing.

Another glaring issue in this theory: could Holmes have even been in Whitechapel during the times of the murders? We know that at the time the Ripper murders were committed he had just started his construction on the "Murder Castle". We also know at that time he was struggling in legal battles with several of the construction companies because of nonpayment. The first such lawsuit was in 1888. In his day steam engine travel was relatively new, with the first ships equipped sailing in 1845. This would cut down the time of international travel to between five and fourteen days. However, spending months in London while you have an active construction site and pending court cases seems implausible at best. Holmes may have traveled to London before or after the Jack the Ripper murders, but the time they began would have been the worst time in his life to disappear.

The foremost expert on Holmes, Adam Selzer, is a Chicago historian, author, and tour guide. He is the author of the definitive biography *H.H. Holmes: The True History of the White City Devil*. Within his works, he gives irrefutable evidence as to why Holmes cannot be Jack the Ripper. First, Chicago voting records prove that he voted in the election in November 1888. He could not be in London killing Mary Kelly, while he was voting in Chicago in early November. The second item of note is the birth of Holmes' daughter, which was on July 4th, 1889. Coincidentally, that event happened ninety-one years, to the day, before the birth of your author. This also means that the child would have been conceived in October or November 1888, right in the middle of Jack the Ripper's killing spree. It is impossible for Holmes to be in London while conceiving a child in Chicago.

Legend: Holmes Faked His Death

The other claim that Jeff Mudgett makes in his book is that his great-great-grandfather found a way to escape execution and put a cadaver in his place. This legend has been around since the time of his execution and the special instructions for his burial only helped fuel the fire. Holmes requested to be buried encased in concrete. Naturally, people thought that he paid people off so he could escape to South America or Europe. It could have also been because Holmes was such a prolific grave robber himself, he knew that people would try to dig him up to steal anything they could get their hands on or do any of the number of horrible things he had done to other people's remains.

The popularization of this legend became so popular in modern times that they actually dug up his grave in 2017. They would finally answer the questions around the legend of Holmes being able to escape death. What they found was incredible. They dug ten feet down to find an empty wooden box. This box had a false front, that was meant to fool anyone who had gotten that deep into thinking the grave was empty. Just a few inches deeper they found cement that would be chipped away to find the coffin inside. The body in the coffin was well preserved, he even had his signature mustache. They took DNA and ran the tests, checking it against the DNA they had from Jeff Mudgett. When the test results came back, they found that the body in the coffin was indeed related to Jeff. With that they could positively conclude that H.H. Holmes was buried in the coffin. There is no way that he could have faked his death, and a 130-year-old question was answered. However, Jeff Mudgett has remained unconvinced and has accused the laboratory of bias and wants an additional DNA test. To date this has not been done, but I do not believe the result would be any different. The person in the coffin ten feet down and encased in concrete was none other than Holmes himself.

Expand Your Mind

Podcasts
- *Murder Metal Mayhem* - Ep. 205 – "H.H. Holmes: Murdering Con Man"
- *TimeSuck w/ Dan Cummins* - Ep. 25 – "Serial Killer H.H. Holmes and his Murder Castle"
- *Last Podcast on the Left* - Eps. 200-203
- *Killer Psyche* – "H.H. Holmes: The Truth Behind the Murder Castle"

Books
- *Devil in the White City* by Erik Larson
- *Depraved* by Harold Schechter
- *The Strange Case of Dr. H.H. Holmes* Edited by John Borowski
- H.H. Holmes: The True History of the White City Devil by Adam Selzer

Documentaries
- *H.H. Holmes America's First Serial Killer* (2004) - A John Borowski Film
- *American Ripper* (2017)

CHAPTER FOUR

LIZZIE BORDEN

I am very aware that Lizzie Borden is not even classified as a serial killer nor was she even convicted of any crime. If she were convicted, she would have been classified as a family annihilator. However, the Borden case is one of the most famous and long-lasting true crime cases of all time, and I feel like it is worth taking the time to dispel the myths.

Lizzie was born into a wealthy family who lived in Fall River, Massachusetts. They lived in the center of the industrial area of Fall River and not on "the Hill," which was where the wealthiest people lived. If the stories are to be believed her father was a bit of a miser and would not spend his money. They had no indoor plumbing and would often have to scrounge for food. They were also a very religious family and attended the Central Congregational Church.

Lizzie's mother passed away in 1863, when Lizzie was just three years old. Her father remarried three years later to Abby Gray, when she would only be six years old. Lizzie believed that Abby had married her father for his wealth and would only call her Mrs. Borden. In the court accounts, it was stated that both Lizzie and her sister Emma seemed distant from their parents and rarely ate with them.

In May of 1892, Lizzie was thirty-two years old. There is a story that she had built a roost for some pigeons on the property with the hope of keeping them as pets. Her father would go and kill the pigeons with a hatchet because he believed it was encouraging the boys in the neighborhood to break into his barn and hunt the pigeons, themselves. It is said that Lizzie was very upset, and this may have been the final straw. Just a few months later in July, the climate in the home was so bad that both Lizzie and her sister would take a trip to New Bedford, and returned just one week before the murders.

The real story behind the tension in the house had all to do with money. Andrew Borden had been paying lots of attention to his wife's family and giving them both money and real estate. The two sisters were very angry that their inheritance was being given away and it seemed that it would all come to a head at some point. In fact, a few weeks before the murders the whole family was violently ill. Abby even feared that they had been poisoned because Andrew was not well liked around town.

The infamous day would be August 4th, 1892. Andrew went on his morning walk at 9:00 a.m. and returned around 10:30 a.m. During that time Abby faced the killer. She would initially be struck on the side of the head with a hatchet causing her to fall face down on the floor. After seventeen more blows to the back of her head with the hatchet, she did not survive the encounter. When Andrew returned, he had trouble getting in the front door and was forced to knock. The maid unlocked the door and said that she heard Lizzie laughing from the second floor. Lizzie would deny the claim. Andrew then lay down for a nap on the couch. Just before 11:10 a.m. Lizzie yelled up to the maid that someone had come in and father had been killed. Andrew was struck ten or eleven times with a hatchet in the head. The doctor, who lived just across the street, would determine that it happened while he was asleep and that it was very recent, and the police wrote in their report that the murder of Andrew Borden took place at 11:00 a.m.

Lizzie would be interviewed by the police at the scene, but her answers were contradictory. In their report, they noted that they disliked her attitude, but they did not check her for any physical evidence. Lizzie would tell them that she was feeling sick, and they left without doing a proper search of the property. This caused a lot of criticism toward the police later on. They did, however, find two hatchets, two axes, and a hatchet with a broken handle in the basement, but neglected to remove any of them from the house as evidence. Later, during the autopsies, the bodies of Andrew and Abby were checked for poisons, and none were found.

On August 5th the police did a more thorough search and finally took the broken handled hatchet. That evening they let Lizzie know that she was a suspect in the murders and the very next day she would be seen destroying a dress. She claimed that there was paint on the dress, but most people believed that it was blood-stained clothing.

Lizzie was arrested on August 11th and officially indicted on December 2nd. The trial would begin on June 5th, 1893. Just a few days before, on June 1st, there was another axe murder in Fall River. The circumstances were very similar and may have really swayed the jurors. It wasn't until 1894 that the murderer was found, convicted, and determined not to have been in the vicinity during the Borden murders. On June 20th, 1893, Lizzie Borden was acquitted of all charges and set free. Lizzie passed away at the age of sixty-six from pneumonia on June 1, 1927. Her sister Emma died just nine days later while living in a nursing home. The sisters would never marry and would never avoid the stigma of the brutal murder of their parents.

Myth #1: Lizzie Was a Shoplifter

There is a story that crops up from time to time that Lizzie Borden was a kleptomaniac and was always getting in trouble for stealing from the stores in Fall River. It is said that her father always paid her debt and covered up her indiscretions. Whenever I hear this story, it makes me think of Winona Ryder and the stories of her stealing in the 90s. There are many different reasons someone might shoplift, the obvious one being that they need to steal to survive. However, this was not the case for either Lizzie or Winona. Since both of them had all the money that they would ever need, they would steal for a psychological reason. Often it is just the pure thrill of stealing, which is why it is often very small things. They get a certain satisfaction from getting away with something naughty and the excitement of the event will give them enough of a high that they need to continue doing it.

These stories seem to have come to light shortly after the murders in 1897. After the trial and the acquittal, the Borden family was talked about mercilessly, and their reputation was destroyed. One story that is cited often is about two missing pieces of painted porcelain that were taken from a jewelry store called Tilden-Thurber Co, a store that Lizzie was known to shop in. A woman came into the store with a piece of porcelain that needed to be repaired and stated that Lizzie had given it to her as a gift. The store called the police and when they went to the house to question Lizzie, they found the other piece of missing porcelain. Lizzie would say that she had purchased the artwork and had given a piece to her friend. Ultimately, the store dropped the charges, and nothing would come of it. The media would later latch on to this story, and people began talking about Lizzie's history of kleptomania. However, there are no reliable sources or accounts of any theft done by Lizzie Borden.

Of course, this doesn't mean that Lizzie was not a kleptomaniac. Although he often helped her out when she was in trouble, it was known that her father kept a tight rein on the family's money. It is one of the main theories for why he was killed as this may have even been a bone of contention between them. So, it is possible that daddy dearest would not buy Lizzie the finer things that she wanted, and she would resort to stealing them. Eventually, he may have even tired of always being accused of wrongdoing because of his daughter and threatened to cut her off, which may have led directly to his death. We will never truly know; we can only theorize and guess at the reasoning.

Myth #2: Lizzie Attempted to Poison Her Family

It has become well-known that for a few weeks prior to the murders, Lizzie was talking about the possibility that someone was trying to poison their family. Could this have been because of their wealth or some business dealing? Was there another party that wanted the Borden family out of the way so they could have what they had? Or was it Lizzie, already planning the demise of her family, and spreading the rumor to give herself an alibi to cover her true intent?

We have already established that the whole family was sick for a few weeks before the murders. It was also proven that no poison was found in their system at the autopsy. So, was it really just bad meat that caused the family to be sick or was it an attempt by Lizzie to take out her stepmother and father? Eli Bence, the local druggist, testified that Lizzie came into the drug store the day before the murders to obtain prussic acid (hydrogen cyanide). He had refused her request because she didn't have a prescription and she would argue that she had gotten it before and only needed it to clean her sealskin cape. This testimony was thrown out, even though there was other evidence that she had gone elsewhere to try to buy the prussic acid, unsuccessfully. When reading the testimony, it's also confirmed that prussic acid was not commonly used in cleaning sealskin. I had to look up the uses for prussic acid, mostly because I have never used it for anything, and I currently own no sealskin and would have no idea how to clean it if I did. Oddly enough, I could not find any uses for it for cleaning, however I did find many uses for it as a highly toxic poison. It has been used as a pest repellent and has been widely used in chemical weapons.

So, then the question seems to be, why would Lizzie have any use for picking up prussic acid in the first place, if not to kill her parents? If it is the case that Lizzie was spreading these rumors as an alibi, would it have worked? During that time, it was not uncommon for women to use poison to kill their family members. Often, they would kill multiple members of their family before ever being caught. Before the turn of the century, forensics was definitely not what it is now and the probability that a woman could get away with a poisoning was pretty high. Here is another question to ponder: when Lizzie was unable to purchase the prussic acid, why didn't she buy rat poison or any of the other hundreds of legal poisons she get could her hands on?

It seems to me that Lizzie may have tried to poison her parents and inadvertently poisoned the whole family with some makeshift poison. When this didn't work, she then decided to get her hands on the real stuff, but when she was unable to obtain any, she decided to go the old fashion route and kill them with her trusty hatchet. The interesting thing is this all leads to the belief that Lizzie must have had a very specific timeline for killing her parents. The prussic acid would kill them very quickly and she had little time to poison them over an extended period. The poison that she had already used had not worked over several days, so the hatchet would have been a very final and immediate solution. Were there big changes coming for the family that Lizzie needed to stop before they went into motion? Was her father going to disown her and leave her without a penny? These are all questions that we will never know the answers to, but it makes the case intriguing.

Myth #3: Lizzie Was a Lesbian and Killed Her Parents Because They Found Out

The idea that Lizzie Borden was a lesbian has been a theory since the beginning. The fact that both she and her sister never married was a scandal in their lifetime. This was a time in our history when a woman's role was to find a man, get married, and take care of their family. The life that Lizzie lived, even before the murders, was an unusual one for the times. She was thirty-two years old, still living with her parents with no prospects for marriage, when the murders happened. There was a scandal that was reported on October 10th, 1892, by the Fall River Globe, where Lizzie Borden was pregnant out of wedlock. However, two days later the paper would retract the article and release an apology, stating it was false and only an unsavory detective who had tricked their reporter with the story. Over the years there were many other stories that were reported of Lizzie having male suitors, but none of them ever came to any real revelation. In fact, there are many letters written by Lizzie refuting any claims that the papers would make.

It didn't help that after the murders her sister, Emma, would move out and never speak to her again. The tale is that Emma got angry because of a romantic relationship that Lizzie had with an actress, Nance O'Neill, who was a proud lesbian. Of course, the only evidence for this is a letter that Emma wrote stating that she left the home because of events at a dinner party, which she would not reveal. She also mentions that she went to the family spiritual adviser and was told to go live someplace else. This is not hard evidence, by any means, but it shows that there may have been some activity going on that would have had serious moral implications during their time period, like homosexual behavior. There is also some evidence that a man named Lizzie Borden as a cause for his impending divorce, in the legal documents. Could it be that Lizzie made his wife fall in love with her and caused the breakup of their marriage?

This theory and its implications in the murder of her stepmother and father starts with their devout religious upbringing. The family was very Christian, and they were part of many of the local Christian societies, but whether this was for status or actual devotion is also up for debate. Was the family prepared for more scandal or the religious and societal implications if this came out to the public? Could this have led to Lizzie's father disowning her and cutting her out of the inheritance? Judging by the fact that this is still a very real possibility for people coming out of the closet today, it is not a stretch to believe that they would have done the same thing in the 1890s.

The story is that Lizzie and Bridget Sullivan (aka Maggie), the family maid, had a sexual relationship. If this is true or not, is it really motive for murder? If you believe that Andrew was both physically and sexually abusive to his children, it might be. Again, there is no real evidence that there was ever a relationship between Lizzie and Bridget. However, there is an account of Bridget Sullivan mentioning that she lied on the stand to protect Lizzie. So, was she protecting a lover? A friend? Or just a girl that she had cared for? We may never know why Bridget protected Lizzy, but it certainly gives us room for speculation. There have been several recent movies that have tried to shed light on some of those theories. Our pop culture is exactly what grows the mythology around these historical figures; the

more real it seems, the easier it is to influence our opinion
on what actually happened.

Legend: Lizzie Borden's Ghost & Dark Tourism

Of my many pursuits outside the truth of serial killers, one is delving into the paranormal side of things. There may even be plans to merge the true crime with the paranormal in the near future. The idea that these crimes may have been so horrific that they may leave a significant imprint on the locations where they happened is fascinating. This could certainly be true in the case of Lizzie Borden.

Since 1996, the Lizzie Borden House in Falls River, Massachusetts has been open as a museum and bed and breakfast. Sadly, I have not had the pleasure of spending the night in a location that is always included on lists of the top haunted hotels in America. I am looking forward to changing that with a trip to Salem and a stop at the infamous Lizzie Borden House in the future. Since it has been open, there have been reports of many ghostly sightings from lights flickering, doors opening and closing on their own, the sound of laughing children, and the ever-elusive, full-body apparition. It is believed that Abby, Andrew, Lizzie, and even two children who were killed next door by their mother in 1848, now call the residence home.

The tour company U.S. Ghost Adventures acquired the house in 2021 and has continued to ramp up dark tourism with tours, ghost hunts, overnight stays, and pub crawls. This has given new life to the story of the Borden family and a renewed interest. Paranormal fans come from far and wide to catch a glimpse of a ghost from the Borden family. Although some people may believe that this kind of attention detracts or gives this horrible crime attention that it doesn't deserve, I believe that dark tourism is a necessary part of connecting with history. This brings history to life and allows us to interact with it in a whole new way. This doesn't mean that we are celebrating the crimes, but rather remembering the events that have shaped our world and lives. To me, there is little difference between this and going to the battlefield in Gettysburg.

Aside from the Dark Tourism aspects of the Lizzie Borden House, which you should definitely visit (to book go to Lizzie-Borden.com), there are many ghost stories and experiences that people have had at that location. There have been several visits by big-name paranormal investigation teams, the most prominent being Ghost Adventures, who featured the hotel in Season Five, Episode Nine. The team brought in two ladies to try to communicate with the spirits and they would receive some very controversial messages. They also got many spirit box voices and an anger that seems to still linger at the location. This anger would make them physically sick, and they had to stop the investigation altogether. Is this hype just for the show, or an actual account of what can happen when you empty the building and focus an investigation to find the truth? For any of you who have done a public ghost hunt, it is very different than a private investigation. Often the gathering of so many people and the varying intents of the people attending will change the energy of the location and give you little to no results. It is much different when you are locked in a place with a small team of people who are all attuned and experienced to investigate the claims.

The claims of ghostly haunting at the Lizzie Borden house include an entity wandering the halls that is believed to be Abby Borden just going about her daily chores. She is said to be seen in the second-floor hallway and guest room. Andrew Borden seems to have been caught as a ghostly visage in the mirror of the dining room. There have been reports of hearing Lizzie's ghost crying in her room and from the room next door. There has also been an account of seeing Lizzie on the stairs, ascending to begin the murder of Abby. Whether you think this is possible or not, it is a fascinating part of our true crime history that many people love to investigate. There are many people that believe that by interacting with these ghostly apparitions we can finally figure out the full story of what happened on that fateful day. However, it seems that none of the paranormal teams have been able to get a clearer picture of who actually killed Abby and Andrew.

Expand Your Mind

Podcasts
- *Murder Metal Mayhem* - Ep. 233 – "Lizzie Borden: Axin' No Questions"
- *TimeSuck w/ Dan Cummins* - Ep. 108 – "Lizzie Borden Took an Axe…"
- *Last Podcast on the Left* - Eps. 475, 476
- *Killer Psyche* – "Lizzie Borden"

Books
- *Lizzie Borden: The Legend, the Truth, the Final Chapter* by Arnold Brown
- *Forty Whacks: New Evidence in the Life and Legend of Lizzie Borden* by David Kent

Documentaries
- *The Curse of Lizzie Borden* (2022)
- "The Strange Case of Lizzie Borden" (2005) - *History's Mysteries*
- *Ghost Adventures* (2011) Season 5 Ep. 5 – "Lizzie Borden House"

CHAPTER FIVE

ED GEIN

He may not be the most well-known killer in this book, but he may well be the most influential in pop culture. No other killer has inspired as many movie franchises as the Butcher of Plainfield. Norman Bates from *Psycho*, Leatherface from *The Texas Chainsaw Massacre*, and Buffalo Bill from *The Silence of the Lambs* were all inspired by his story. The account of the life of Ed Gein is so strange and what they found in his barn was so macabre that it has influenced the way we think about modern horror.

Just ten years, and a couple of hundred miles to the north, after Holmes would swing on the hangman's noose Ed Gein was born. His father was an alcoholic, and his mother was extremely religious. She would constantly read scripture and preach to Ed and his brother about the evils of the world, especially dealing with women. In her eyes, she was the only pure woman and everyone else was promiscuous, and would lead them into sin.

Ed had very little social interaction with anyone outside of the Gein farm. His only time away from his mother and father was when he was at school. Even at school, Ed was the weird kid. He had very few friends and when he would make friends, his mother would punish him for it.

In 1940, when Ed was thirty-four, his father passed away from heart failure. It would now be up to Ed and his brother to bring in the money. The brothers both did odd jobs as handymen around the community. Ed would also babysit for many of the families. Henry, Ed's brother, eventually wanted to move out and would often talk badly about their mother and her constant chiding about his lifestyle. On May 16th, 1944, Ed was burning some vegetation in their marsh and the fire got out of control, leading to the fire department eventually coming to put it out. Later that night Ed reported his brother missing. They found Henry lying face down in the marsh. Since he was not burned and there were no other obvious injuries they officially listed it as asphyxiation. There was always speculation that Ed killed his brother, possibly over an argument relating to their mother.

Not long after the death of Henry, Ed's mother had a stroke, and he would then have to take care of her full-time. About a year later, she had another stroke and shortly after, on December 29th, 1945, she passed away. Her death would destroy Ed and lead him into madness. He was now all on his own, with a farm to continue to maintain. He continued to do handyman work to keep money coming in. He also boarded up all the rooms used by his mother and left them untouched. Now that his mother was gone and he had no one to monitor him, he began consuming stories about cannibals and people making things from human skin.

From the time of his mother's death in 1945 until November 16th, 1957, when Ed was arrested, he lived as the quiet strange guy in town. He would hang out in town at the local bars and businesses. It seemed that everyone knew him and wrote him off as the lonely sad case at the edge of town. On December 8th, 1954, Mary Hogan, the manager of a tavern, disappeared only leaving an overturned chair, a blood stain, and a spent cartridge from a .32 caliber pistol. Later they would find the matching gun in Ed's home. Just three years later, on November 16th, 1957, Bernice Worden, the Plainfield hardware store owner, would also turn up missing. Her son was a deputy sheriff and when he visited the store that morning, he found the register open and a bloodstain on the floor. Ed was the last person to see her, buying a gallon of antifreeze that morning. Ed went out to the grocery store that evening, where the police would come and arrest him. No one was prepared for what they would find at the farm that night.

In the barn, they found the decapitated body of Worden, hung upside down and dressed out like a deer. They were able to determine that she had been shot with a .22 rifle and the mutilation was done after her death. They also found assorted bones and bone fragments. They found several pieces of furniture made of human skin, including two chairs, a lampshade, and a wastebasket. On his bedposts, they found human skulls. He had several bowls made from human skulls. The police found a corset, leggings, a nipple belt, and several masks all made from human skin. Nine vulvae were found in a shoebox. Mary Hogan's skull was in a box and Bernice Worden's head was in a burlap sack. Lastly, Worden's heart would be found in a plastic bag in front of his stove.

After this grisly discovery, they would finally interrogate Ed. He would then tell them a five-year tale of graverobbing, while in a fugue state. He would take the recently deceased bodies home and skin them for all of his projects. He would claim to have visited over forty graves to rob but confirmed that he only stole from nine graves. When they went to investigate the gravesites and found that Ed was true to his word; many of the bodies were either completely missing or parts had been removed. He also confessed to attempting to create a "woman suit." He wanted to become his mother, completely. Ed would take his "woman suit," including a woman's scalp, face, vest that included breasts, and female genitalia, and dance in the moonlight of a full moon as a ceremony. He confessed to the murder of Mary Hogan but could not remember the details. When asked if he had sex with the bodies, Ed would deny any sexual engagement saying that they smelled too bad. Before the end of this first interrogation, Sheriff Art Schley would lose his cool and bang Ed's face into the brick wall, causing the testimony to be inadmissible in court.

Ed went to trial on November 21st, 1957, and plead not guilty by reason of insanity. He was found mentally incompetent and placed in the Central State Hospital for the Criminally Insane. Eventually, he was transferred to Mendota State Hospital where the doctors would determine Ed sane enough to stand trial in 1968. So, Ed was back in a courtroom on November 7th, 1968. He was found guilty of the murder of Bernice Worden, but in a second trial, he would again be found to be criminally insane and committed to a mental hospital. He would live the rest of his life there as a model patient, who was well liked, until he passed away from respiratory failure and lung cancer on July 26th, 1984.

Myth #1: Ed Was a Cannibal

In many of the movies inspired by Ed, we find characters who feasted on their victims. As children, we are all afraid of the monster under the bed or the monster in the shadows because we know it's going to eat us. This has become part of our cultural mythology. Gein would be thought of as an American monster and when his crimes were discovered the reality was far scarier than the fantasy. The bowls made from skulls, the skin chairs and lampshades, and the gutted body of Bernice Worden hanging like a deer all led to the belief that Gein was eating his victims, which is a horrifying thought.

Ed was a fifty-one-year-old man, living on a farm, that supplied meat to many people in the community. He would often bring deer meat to his fellow neighbors. He was also seen as mild-mannered and always willing to lend a helping hand. As the story of Ed Gein was popularized in his community, he became the bogeyman in the shadows. The people would hear of the horrors of the barn and vomit, remembering eating the meat that Ed had given them, believing it to be the meat of his victims. No one could believe that he would have so many body parts available to him and not eat them. In some of the early news media reports, they would mention that Bernice Worden's heart was found in a pan on the stove. This single report would fuel the belief that Ed Gein was indeed a cannibal. Although this is a pretty easy conclusion to come to, the truth seems to be much more bizarre.

It is interesting to note that the officers in Plainfield, who discovered the macabre scene, had very little formal training as police officers. The sheriff himself had only been an officer for a month at the time of the investigation. The myth was started by District Attorney Kileen when he answered the media saying that he believed it must be cannibalism. As Harold Schecter investigated the evidence for his book, *Deviant,* and reviewed the police reports, he found that the heart, while in front of the stove, was not in a pan but in a plastic bag. Ed was questioned about his intentions with the heart. He told them that he intended to burn the heart and other parts of the body that he could not use for his projects. He denied ever eating any human flesh or any parts of his victims and would continue to say that until the day that he died. The community would still be scared about the venison that Ed gave them, fearing it was really human meat. However, it seems that the lore about Ed being a cannibal was nothing more than parents trying to scare their children into behaving and overzealous law enforcement guessing at the possibilities.

Even more bizarre than the story of cannibalism is the idea that Gein was looking to recreate his mother. He would collect body parts from his grave robberies and killings to create a substitute for his mother. This would give rise to the idea of the woman suit, made famous by the movie, *The Silence of the Lambs*. I am not sure which is worse, the fact that he may have been making a woman suit to become his mother or that he just wanted a figure that looked like his mother. His obvious obsession with his mother, his low-functioning mindset, and being left alone to his own devices created the perfect storm for a psychotic killer.

Myth #2: Ed Was a Serial Killer

At the time that Gein's crimes were discovered, the term serial killer was not even coined yet. He was only convicted of killing one person, Bernice Worden, but he would also confess to the murder of Mary Hogan. Under the traditional classification of a serial killer, requiring three or more murders with a cooling-off period between each, Ed would not meet the qualifications. The new standard is two or more with a cooling-off period between each, and Ed would fit the requirement under this new standard. Of course, I would agree with Stephen Giannangelo, in his book *Real Life Monsters*, that the standard should be changed to incorporate intent when we are classifying a serial murderer. Many people would be serial murderers if they weren't caught after the first kill or even before. The good news is our forensics have become so good that the age of the serial killer has been severely limited.

However, was this the extent of Ed's crimes? Did he only kill two women and rob up to nine graves? The truth is Gein was also suspected of several disappearances, for which he was never tried. Also, it seems that they would find remains in the barn from many more than the nine victims he claimed to have dug up at the cemetery. Of course, this doesn't mean that Gein killed any more than two people, even if it does prove that he robbed more graves than previously thought. However, in the barn, they found a young girl's dress and several body parts of two young girls, determined to be about fifteen years old. They have never been able to identify these two people, but they were able to determine that they didn't match any of the graves that Ed was believed to have robbed.

With that information, it is possible that he killed at least two more people in addition to Worden and Hogan. There are six other people who disappeared under strange circumstances, where circumstantial evidence may point toward Ed Gein being the culprit. Although he would never confess to any other murders, it is certainly possible that Gein may have had ten or more victims. It will always be up for debate as to whether these additional victims were alive or already dead when Gein acquired them. However, it is almost certain that Gein was a serial killer, and if nothing else he was definitely a mentally disturbed and psychotic murderer.

Myth #3: Ed Was the First Transgender Psycho Killer

This theory is a more recent idea that comes from the demonizing of people in the LGBTQ+ community throughout history. Sadly, this continues today, and we have people who believe that those who choose to live differently are sexually deviant or pedophiles. This could not be further from the truth. Let me start off by saying that I support all people's rights and am an ally for the LGBTQ+ community. I do not think Ed would have considered himself trans, even if he knew what it was. I think to understand if Ed Gein was transgender, we need to understand what's defined as transgender first. The GLADD website states, "Transgender is a term used to describe people whose gender identity differs from the sex they were assigned at birth." This is not to be confused with cross-dressing, or otherwise temporarily disguising or masquerading as a member of the other sex.

When we look at Ed's life, there was never any indication that he identified with any other gender than male. He was a diagnosed schizophrenic and necrophile. Necrophilia, an obsession or attraction to corpses, has varying degrees. Ed was attracted to dead bodies but would deny having sex with any of the dead bodies or his victims, his entire life. It seems from all the evidence, that he did not want to become a woman; instead, he wanted to become his mother. He struggled with a serious psychological over-identification with the only woman that he loved, and who loved him.

He held her in such high esteem that she was perfection, and if he wanted to obtain that perfection, he would need to become her.

I do not believe that Ed Gein was transgender. I do believe he was a psychologically disturbed person, who loved his mother and was unable to receive the psychological treatment or care to help him with his trauma. I also believe that these murders have no connection to the transgender or LGBTQ+ community at all. I know that there are all sorts of people who create stigma around the transgender community because it has become a hot-button topic, just as the larger LGBTQ+ community was before it. That is not to say there are not still people who believe horrible things about others whether it is their sexual orientation, their gender identity, or their skin color; it has continued to run rampant in our society. Sadly, we often live in communities that are very close-minded and refuse to show true unconditional love to the people around them. We would all be better off if we could learn to love the people around us and allow people to live safe, fulfilling lives however and with whomever they choose.

Legend: Ed Has Inspired Our Horror Movie Characters

In 1957, Ed Gein was arrested for the crimes discovered in his barn in Plainfield, Wisconsin. The story immediately gripped our horror community. He was certainly not the first killer, but the story was so outlandish that horror movies would never be the same. Our horror community will often say that fictional horror characters are just fine because they are not real. I would argue that most, if not all, "fictional" killers were inspired by real ones, which makes them even more dangerous. If it is true that our thoughts create our reality and our brain doesn't know the difference between "truth" and "belief," why would we think that real or "fictional" matters? I love horror, not because I like to be scared or love gore, but because I love the artistry and what it says about our current culture. You can truly learn a ton from what people find terrifying. Although horrific, I love true crime, because it is the "truth" about what scares us and provides awareness and protection from the evil that lives in our world.

The story of Ed Gein would inspire movies from the time the report hit the headlines. It can be argued that he has inspired every horror movie character in some way and several common horror movie tropes. Any movie that mentions grave robbing, cannibalism, the dismembering and keeping of body parts, and creating items from human flesh all share their lineage from the crimes of Ed Gein. It is fascinating that this strange, quiet, and mild-mannered farmer from Plainfield would have such wide-reaching effects on pop culture. The following are eleven movies that were directly influenced by Ed Gein.

Psycho (1960)

The Alfred Hitchcock classic would be released just three years after the crimes were discovered in Plainfield. The movie was an adaptation of the novel written in the 50s by Robert Bloch. The author just happened to live a few towns away from Plainfield, Wisconsin but knew nothing about the crimes of Ed Gein when he wrote the novel. However, when Hitchcock adapted the story for the movie, he would make some direct allusions to the, now infamous, Ed Gein crimes. Norman Bates would be so obsessed with his mother that he would begin killing women, keeping parts of the dead, and dressing up like his mother. These are all taken directly from the account of Gein. This movie would inspire a whole series of films and a television show. There would even be a remake in 1998, starring Vince Vaughn as Norman Bates.

Three on a Meathook (1972)

This movie would draw its influence from Gein in a new way. In the movie, several girls meet their end after meeting a young man who lives in the woods with his deranged father. The son was completely obedient to his father, a slight difference from Gein being completely obedient to his mother. This movie is loosely based on Gein, but the influence is definitely there.

Deranged (1974)

Deranged is a cult classic movie that lovers of gritty independent films know and love. This movie has some incredible special effects done by the legendary Tom Savini himself. The killer in this film is completely based on Ed Gein. He is a grave robber, who kills after the death of his overbearing religious mother and collects the skin of his victims. The full title of this film is *Deranged: Confessions of a Necrophile*, which we have already stated is true about Ed, knowing the definition of necrophilia.

The Texas Chainsaw Massacre (1974)

This is another film that makes the all-time classic horror movie list and is directly inspired by the crimes of Gein. The killer, named Leatherface who was played by Gunner Hansen, was directly derived from Gein and the skin masks he would wear. One of the co-writers of the film, Kim Henkel, would admit that she studied the story of Gein for the film and thought that it might be fun if the whole family were in on the crimes. This franchise continues to inspire further movies and sequels to this day.

Motel Hell (1980)

This film was more directly inspired by movies like *Psycho* and *Texas Chainsaw Massacre*, but that would all lead back to the original true account of Ed Gein. "It takes all kinds of Critters to make Farmer Vincent's Fritters," and "Meat's meat and man's gotta eat," are two lines from this incredible movie. The protagonists are a brother and sister duo that are killing random people to use in their famous sausage-making business. Go get yourself some of Farmer

Vincent's Fritters, and you'll feel just like one of Ed's neighbors.

The Silence of the Lambs (1991)

This movie spawned sequels and a television franchise that has been excellent. The main killer in this film, Hannibal Lecter, was not based on Gein but has still become one of our legendary horror movie characters. The killer that is, however, inspired by Gein is Buffalo Bill. Bill would choose women of his liking, kill them, and skin them all to make a woman suit that he would wear and sexually fantasize about being a woman. By the end of the movie, Hannibal would even wear the face of a victim to escape, taking a move from Gein. The movie was adapted from a series of novels by Thomas Harris.

Ed and His Dead Mother (1993)

This is a little-known film that was only released in one theater and stars Steve Buscemi as Ed Chilton. Ed loved his overbearing mother so much that he brought her back from the dead. As a zombie, he needs to get her flesh to eat and starts killing women to feed them to his mother. It is obvious that this horror-comedy is based directly on the account of Ed Gein.

Ed Gein (2000)

This would be the first movie that would directly feature the story of Ed Gein. It would also inspire several other serial-killer-centric movies, *Dahmer* (2002) and *Gacy* (2003). Most of the movie is based on the actual account of Gein's crimes, but just like anything produced in Hollywood, they would take a few creative liberties. There are scenes of Gein cannibalizing the corpses that he acquired, which of course he says he never did.

House of 1000 Corpses (2003)

This movie was Rob Zombie's masterpiece and took lots of pieces from true crime lore. Ed Gein is specifically featured in several parts including an exhibit in Captain Spaulding's Murder Ride. Then there is the skin-wearing psycho that is closely related to the skin-wearing of Gein, himself. There are also lots of parallels between this film and *Texas Chainsaw Massacre*. This movie inspired two sequels that continued the story of the family and Otis B. Driftwood, the character inspired by Ed Gein.

Ed Gein: The Butcher of Plainfield (2007)

This horror movie has little resemblance to the actual Gein account and prefers to use the name while taking creative liberties, making Gein into the stuff of nightmares. The giant of a man, Kane Hodder, famous for his role as Jason Voorhees in the *Friday the 13th* franchise, plays Ed Gein. This would be a complete divergence from the real Ed Gein, who was a small, quiet man. Although the movie is not accurate, it is definitely inspired by the account of Ed Gein.

Texas Chainsaw Massacre (2022)

Although the name stays the same this movie is not a remake of the original. It takes place 50 years after the original and continues the story of Leatherface. The family is gone, and it is now just him and his surrogate mother.

Leatherface has again built an obsessive love for his mother and when she dies, carnage ensues. The ideas of wearing the skin mask and the love of his mother all point back to the original account of Ed Gein.

These movies were all inspired by Gein and countless more have been inspired by them. The lineage of our horror movies is filled with inspiration from true crime. Ghostface from the *Scream* franchise was inspired by the real-life case of Danny Rolling the Gainesville Ripper. *Wolf Creek* (2005) was inspired by the backpack murder of Ivan Milat. *The Clovehitch Killer* (2018) was inspired by the real-life killer Dennis Rader. *The Strangers* (2008) is based on the life and crimes of the Manson Family. *The Frozen Ground* (2013) is based on the serial killer Robert Hansen. Fritz Haarman would inspire the 1931 movie *M* and the 1973 movie *The Tenderness of Wolves*. These are just a few of the killers that have inspired films, there have also been countless films and documentaries about the serial killers themselves.

Our idea of horror has always come from the real-life cases that have inspired them. However, our horror community often believes that talking about the real inspiration for our "movie" killers is a little too close to home. To shrug that off and disparage the real historical accounts is a mistake in my eyes. I think we need to embrace both or none at all. With that said, I understand how the true accounts can be much too close for some people to feel comfortable consuming. We all have the right to choose where we spend our time and our money. However, we do not have the right to judge others for the things that they enjoy or take an interest in. The idea that watching true crime glorifies the criminals, but watching a horror movie does not is completely wrong. It seems that creating a "fictional" character from a historical one would be the ultimate glorification. Not to mention, the effect that "fake" violence and murder have on normalizing this behavior in our minds. Whereas seeing the actual horrors seems to have a sobering effect on people, often triggering more empathy.

The crimes of Ed Gein and other real-life killers have shaped and changed the horror genre in unimaginable ways. We will never truly know the reach that these accounts will have for years to come. But one thing is sure, there are crimes happening today that will inspire and change the horror community in the future.

Podcasts

- *Murder Metal Mayhem* - Ep. 163 – "Ed Gein: Nothing Like a Cold One"
- *TimeSuck w/ Dan Cummins* - Bonus Ep. 17 – "Ed Gein: The Butcher of Plainfield"
- *Last Podcast on the Left* - Eps. 172-174
- *Killer Psyche* – "Ed Gein: Hollywood's Favorite Killer"
- *Lil Stinkers* - Ep. 11 – "Ed Gein"

Books

- *The Ed Gein File: A Psycho's Confession and Case Documents* by John Borowski
- *Deviant* by Harold Schechter
- *Unhinged: The Shocking True Story of Ed Gein, the Butcher of Plainfield* by Robert Keller

Documentaries

- *Psycho: The Lost Tapes of Ed Gein* (2023)
- *World's Most Evil Killers* Season 1 Ep. 7

CHAPTER SIX

THE ZODIAC KILLER

This is another killer that we can only speculate upon. The Zodiac has never been caught and there have been no completely compelling theories that have uncovered a credible suspect. Although there have been many that have claimed to crack the ciphers and discover the true identity of this killer, there has been little to no conclusive evidence. I am of the opinion that unless someone finds evidence in their grandfather's attic, we will never truly know who committed these crimes.

Cheri Jo Bates was a freshman at River City College in Riverside, California, and became the first suspected Zodiac victim on October 30th, 1966. The killer would be waiting in a nearby bush for her to go to her car after spending time at the library. He would already have disabled her car, and it is theorized that he first offered her help. Ultimately, he dragged her into the bushes, stabbing her in the back and slashing her throat, nearly decapitating her. A few days later the first letter was sent to the local news. The killer claimed that Cheri was not the first and wouldn't be the last. To add insult to injury the killer would eventually send the same letter to the police and even her father.

Just over two years after the first suspected murder, on December 20th, 1968, two teenagers on a date were shot to death just outside their car, becoming the first definitive Zodiac murder. The Zodiac would fire two warning shots before both David Faraday and Betty Lou Jensen tried to flee from the car. Betty Lou exited the car first, quickly followed by David. David would be shot in the head, almost as soon as he exited the vehicle, while Betty Lou was shot five times in the back as she tried to run from the car. The precision of the shots fired gave rise to the idea that he used a flashlight or was a marksman since the area was pitch black at the time of the murders.

A year and a half would pass before there was another killing. On July 4th, 1969, Michael Mageau and Darlene Farrin would be out for an Independence Day celebration. Early in the night, they would have some concerns about a car following them. Darlene was being harassed by a person called "Paul," although the police would investigate and never identify the mysterious "Paul." The two continued driving and would eventually end up parking at the Blue Rock Springs Park. A car pulled up next to them and opened fire with a 9mm pistol. Michael survived the encounter but was shot four times. Darlene would not survive. She was shot nine times and died on the way to the hospital. Later that night the police received a phone call confessing to the crime and claiming to be the killer of David and Betty Lou.

Three local newspapers received the first of the famous ciphers, each receiving one part, on July 31st, 1969. The cipher was broken a short time later by a high school teacher, who confirmed the message read, "I like killing people because it is so much fun." On August 7th, 1969, another letter would arrive giving the killer a name, "This is the Zodiac speaking…"

Just over a month later, on September 27th, 1969, the Lake Berryessa murder would occur. Bryan Hartnell and Cecilia Shepherd, both twenty years old, were enjoying a picnic lunch at the lake. A man wearing a hood would appear with a gun and claim to be an escaped convict. He tied them up and began stabbing them with a bayonet-sized knife. Bryan was stabbed four times and survived the attack. Cecilia would not survive and suffered fourteen stab wounds to various places on her body. The police would find a note written on the car door claiming several of the murders, leaving behind a crosshair symbol that would become his trademark. The killer also left shoeprints in the sand, identified as military Wing Walkers, sized men's 10.5. The investigators would also believe that the person wearing the shoes was heavyset judging by the impression mark.

The final "officially" attributed murder to the Zodiac would occur on October 11th, 1969. Paul Stine was a cab driver in San Francisco and had given his last ride. He would end up being killed with a 9mm pistol and a gunshot to the head. There were witnesses that saw a man flee the cab after the crime. This is where the famous sketch of the man in glasses would become part of the Zodiac lore. After this murder, there were numerous letters sent to the media and police. The killer would send bloodstained pieces of Paul Stine's shirt and even claimed to pick children off a school bus.

The last known Zodiac incident would occur on March 22nd, 1970. Kathleen Johns, while driving with her infant daughter, was pulled over by another car. He would mention that he noticed that her car had a loose tire and even helped her "fix" the tire. However, he actually loosened the tire, so it would fall off as soon as she tried to drive away. He then offered to drive her to a nearby service station, but instead drove her around threatening to kill her and her daughter. She eventually escaped, hiding in a ditch until he drove away. She reported the abduction to the local police and identified the man from the wanted poster sketch of the Zodiac.

There would be ten more letters sent to the media and police, totaling twenty-one letters. They would each claim an increasingly large body count, although the police would never be able to attribute any other murders to the Zodiac killer. The final letter arrived on April 24th, 1978, just over eleven years after the first murder was recorded. In the years since the speculation and theories have only continued to grow. The body count has gotten as high as 40 murders and although many people have been accused, no one has ever been charged with the crimes. In fact, it remains an open case to this day.

Myth #1: They Have Identified the Zodiac

Since the original crimes were committed there has always been speculation and claims that the Zodiac has been identified. The most recent claim identifying the Zodiac was released to the public in 2021 by the Code Breakers Team, which is a group of several independent investigators from around the world. However, an FBI whistleblower from early 2023 claims that the FBI has positively identified the Zodiac. Although he is still officially only a suspect and has been since 2018, the whistleblower says that Gary Francis Poste is the Zodiac. At forty-seven years after the first "official" killing and over 2,500 suspects, Poste is one of many frontrunners that may actually be the Zodiac. Of course, it is decidedly convenient that Poste was identified as a suspect in 2018, the same year that he died.

The Code Breakers Team provided evidence that they broke the final cipher, which they claim actually names Poste as the killer. As soon as the information was released, many people refuted it. The other main piece of evidence that they provided was that Poste had facial scars that matched the eyewitness accounts of the Zodiac. This might be the weakest piece of evidence that I have ever heard of in a major reveal. First off, we all know that eyewitness reports are widely unreliable, as eyewitnesses often get the details wrong, especially in such a high-tension situation. Not to mention that almost 50 years of hard living could lead to scars for any of us. Much of the evidence they provide sounds plausible, until further investigation, then the case seems to fall apart. They are saying that they may have a partial DNA profile, which could prove or disprove their case, but that evidence hasn't been released.

Over the last nearly fifty years, there has been a multitude of "so-called" positive identifications of the Zodiac. Sadly, none of these have produced any convictions or closed the case. It would be impossible to even do a brief review of all the suspects in this case, but we will touch on a few of the most popular theories, other than the one already described. Tom Voigt is the world's expert on the Zodiac Killer, wrote the book *Zodiac Killer: Just the Facts*, and is the creator of the definitive website on the Zodiac case ZodiacKiller.com. If you need any additional resources or want to do more in-depth research, check out Tom's work. The following is a list of just a few of the most probable suspects.

Richard "Rick" Marshall

- Born on March 13th, 1926, his birthname was Joe Don Dickey. Throughout Rick's life, he would use both names, almost interchangeably. We don't know why he decided to use the Richard Marshall name. He would also use many different birthdates during his lifetime. When he was eighteen years old, he joined the Navy and served for several years. In the late 1960s, Rick moved to the San Francisco Bay area. So, he was in the area and able to commit the crimes. One of the reasons he would end up on the police's radar as the Zodiac killer was that one of the letters from the Zodiac mentioned KTIM. This happened to be the call letters of the radio station where Rick worked as an engineer. This would become further supported by a letter that was mailed to the Los Angeles Times on Rick's 45th birthday. The final piece of "evidence" that the police needed to officially add Rick to the suspect list came in 1976 when he made some suspicious comments over his ham radio. Rick would never be arrested or charged with any wrongdoing in regards to the Zodiac case. However, in 2008, after a tip was given to Tom Voigt by Rick's nurse, the police interviewed Rick. They would determine that Rick was most likely not the Zodiac Killer. Shortly after, Rick Marshall passed away from complications from Parkinson's Disease on September 8th, 2008.

Arthur Leigh Allen

- Born in Hawaii on December 18th, 1933, Arthur was raised in Vallejo, CA. In 1957, he enlisted in the Navy but he was discharged in December of 1958. During that time, he was also arrested for disturbing the peace, but the charges were ultimately dismissed. Allen would then be employed as an elementary school teacher until March 1968, when he was fired for molesting a student. For both his birthday and Christmas in 1968, Allen's mother gave him a Zodiac watch. This watch would have the cross within a circle symbol that became the signature of the Zodiac Killer. He would wear the watch until the police took it as evidence in the Zodiac case.

- In the early 70s, Allen became an official suspect in the Zodiac case. It was determined that the confession letters sent to the media and police after the Bates murder were typed on a Royal model typewriter. In 1991, Allen was served a search warrant and they found a Royal model typewriter, with the correct typeface, in his home. He was also determined to be in the area on the day of the Bates murder. He even took a sick day on November 1st, 1966, the day after the Bates murder occurred.

- Allen allegedly made a confession to his friend Don Cheney, where he described how the Zodiac would kill, in 1969. Allen explained that killing couples at random would make it difficult for the police to catch him. He also mentioned that he wrote letters to the police to throw them off, used a gun with a flashlight taped to the barrel, called himself "Zodiac", and stopped women, claiming that they had tire problems in order to abduct them. The biggest problem with this information is that it matched exactly what the Zodiac did or wrote about in his letters. This information was taken to the police in 1972 and led to a search warrant of his trailer in Santa Rosa, CA, rather than his home in Vallejo, where nothing was found. Additionally, according to family and friends of Allen, he would often use codes and symbols and misspell words to be funny. Many of the phrases that were used in the Zodiac letters were phrases that Allen would use regularly.

- Allen also had the "opportunity" to commit some of the murders, due to his proximal location to the crime scenes. When the Lake Herman Road murders occurred, Allen was living only seven minutes away at his parents' home. During that time of his life, he was drinking heavily and was very depressed after losing his job as a teacher. Similarly, the Blue Rock Springs crime scene was only four minutes away from Allen's home. Mike Mageau, who survived the attack, gave a description of the car the Zodiac was driving. A similar car was owned by Allen's boss, which he had access to and drove from time to time. Mike would also positively identify Allen from a lineup in 1992. Another victim, Darlene Ferrin, was a waitress at a restaurant that Allen frequented and was less than a mile from his house. There is a possibility that they knew one another and may have had some sort of relationship.

- Lake Berryessa was a place where Allen would go camping and scuba diving. Allen would have an alibi for the Zodiac murder that happened there, which never could be substantiated. Allen would actually admit that he planned on going to Lake Berryessa on the day of the murders but went to another location instead. He would also admit that he had bloody knives in his car that day, but they were used to kill a chicken. In the mid-1970s, the survivor of the Lake Berryessa murder, Bryan Hartnell, was taken to Allen's workplace and he would positively identify Allen by both his voice and physical appearance. The footprints left at the scene also matched Allen's shoe size, a men's 10.5.

- In 1991, Ralph Spinelli told the police that just before the murder of Paul Stine, Allen admitted that he was the Zodiac and would go to San Fransico to kill a cabbie to prove it. Of course, this information came twenty-three years after the actual murder took place.

- A potential Zodiac letter that was sent on November 9th, 1969, included a diagram of a bomb. When the police searched Allen's home in 1991, they would find bomb diagrams containing the same ingredients as the letter.

- Allen passed away from diabetes and heart failure on August 26th, 1992. He was fifty-eight years old. The police would obtain another search warrant two days later, but they have never released the results of the search, other than the information that they found a videotape labeled "Z".

Earl Van Best Jr.

- Best was popularized as a Zodiac suspect by the 2014 book by Gary L. Stewart, *The Most Dangerous Animal of All*. In this book, and later a documentary, Stewart claims that his father was the Zodiac killer. Although Stewart was adopted, he would investigate his biological father to discover who his father was. He would find that Best had an interest in ciphers as well as an opera that was mentioned in the Zodiac letters. When Stewart took his father's handwriting samples to an expert, they stated that the Zodiac and Best had similar handwriting. The book paints a compelling argument for Best being the Zodiac. However, the documentary presents the case against Best, as it is built in the book, before demolishing the idea brick by brick. They re-examine the handwriting and determine that it is not very similar, they compare DNA samples and find that it is not consistent with the DNA from the Zodiac letters, and they confirm that Best was not even in the country during the time of the Zodiac murders.

Ted Kaszynski
- Known under another infamous name, the "Unabomber", Kaszynski is one of the more outlandish Zodiac suspects. The only real connection between Ted Kaszynski and the Zodiac is proximity, as Ted was known to be living in San Francisco during the time of the murders. Although they both wrote letters to the media and created bombs, their handwriting is very different and only one of them was ever successful at their bomb-making.

Ted Cruz
- In 2013, an internet meme jokingly referred to Cruz being the Zodiac killer. Since then, there have been many jokes about his appearance and its consistency with the Zodiac sketch. Ted Cruz himself even got in on the fun, posting a cipher on Halloween in 2018. The truth is Cruz was born on December 22nd, 1970, and could not have been the Zodiac killer, since the murders started two years before he was born.

I have always been in the Arthur Leigh Allen camp, myself. I believe that there's insurmountable evidence pointing to Allen as the Zodiac. I know there are many theories out there and everyone has their own ideas, but until there is something definitive, we will never truly know who the Zodiac is.

Myth #2 Zodiac Took Credit for Crimes He Did Not Commit

If there is one thing that we know about criminals, it's that they often lie or at least embellish the truth. Is this the case with the Zodiac? Could he have killed many more, as his letters claimed? Or can we truly believe the rantings of a madman? We know that the definitive killings of the Zodiac only totaled five victims. However, it is believed that the Zodiac kept his own kill tally. In the final letter, believed to be written by the Zodiac, his tally was thirty-seven victims. If you include the victims that survived his attack, as well as the Cheri Jo Bates murder, you would only count eight victims of the Zodiac. So where are the other twenty-nine victims? If you believe that Arthur Leigh Allen was the Zodiac, you may find an answer. Allen ultimately left the San Francisco area in 1971 and moved to Santa Rosa to become a student at Sonoma State University, and in 1972, a series of murders known as the Sonoma hitchhiker murders would begin. In this series of murders, they found seven victims, all females, naked and dumped in rural areas. Up until 1975, they would continue to find bodies, though never officially attributed to the same killer, bringing the Sonoma total to twenty-four victims. If this series of killings was done by the Zodiac killer, that would bring his total up to thirty-two. However, the total claimed by the Zodiac was thirty- seven in 1971, so either the Zodiac was lying about his actual kill tally or there are even more victims that we know nothing about.

Many killers display grandiose thinking and are looking for the infamy that comes with their crimes. This is incredible motivation to inflate the kill count and make their crimes sound much worse than they really were. Many of them will sit in prison after their crimes and the only way that they can get a similar high is through constant retelling to garner any media attention they can get. The Zodiac was never caught but he loved playing a game with the media and police, generating that same feeling of excitement from staying one step ahead. Both Jack the Ripper and Dennis Rader would use similar tactics.

There seem to be an infinite number of theories about who the Zodiac was and the reasons behind why he killed. There is little conclusive evidence to point us in one direction over another. We know that the killer loved to use the media to hype up the crimes that he committed, so it seems unlikely that we could trust anything that he claimed in the letters. The letters themselves are fraught with inconsistencies and may not have even been written by the same people. The one thing that we can be sure of is that he wanted to make himself sound more impressive than he really was. Often these killers are much more self-impressed and use their crimes to fulfill the fantasy that they have of themselves. This has little basis in the reality that you and I live in, and their lives are often sad tales of abuse, drug use, and mental illness.

This leaves us with the enduring question: Is the killer just a liar or are we missing something? There is the possibility that the killer was talking about something else other than a kill count when he mentioned Zodiac thirty-seven, Police zero. Could it be the number of times he evaded the police? The number of times he called the police station? Or the number of donuts he ate after his crimes? Since the killer often wrote in ciphers, we will never really know the truth. I believe it is a safe assumption that he was using this to make himself more famous and spread the fear that he so desperately desired. What is fascinating is that it has worked. We continue to talk about this case and investigate it even though it has remained unsolved for so long. It has become an enduring piece of our true crime history, and thus a part of our modern culture.

Myth #3: The Zodiac Crimes Were Linked to the Manson Family

A book written by Howard Davis, called *The Zodiac/ Manson Connection*, proposed the theory that the Manson family was also responsible for the Zodiac murders. The book talks about a relative of Abigail Folger, who hired a private investigator to investigate the Manson murders. The story is that a source inside the Los Angeles District Attorney's office uncovered that at least one of the Manson family was connected to the Zodiac. This information was concealed because the person involved was already being prosecuted, and they did not want to impede the current trial with new information.

Davis claimed there was information that the Zodiac hood and knife were found in the possession of a male Manson family member, Bruce Davis, who was charged with several murders. However, the trial of Bruce Davis would take place in 1972 and the "source" of Howard's information turned out to be his brother-in-law, who did not work for the DA office until 1974. This means that he could not have been part of any of the Manson family cases. In fact, Vincent Bugliosi, prosecutor and writer of the definitive book on the Manson family *Helter Skelter*, considered the theory to be complete garbage.

The final nail in the coffin for this theory is that when Howard's brother-in-law was asked about the claims he made in the book and the conversations that were supposed to have taken place, his response was, "He's a nutjob" and "It never happened."

Although there are serious inconsistencies in the book and the evidence that is proposed therein, there was a formal investigation into the Manson family and their possible connection with the Zodiac murders. The team that did the investigation ruled out any of the Manson family members as the Zodiac killer. Bruce Davis, specifically, did not match the handwriting or the physical description of the eyewitness accounts of the Zodiac. Bruce was not heavyset and had long hair during the time of the Zodiac murders.

Legend: There Was No Zodiac Killer

The newest documentary to hit Peacock in 2023, *Myth of the Zodiac Killer*, supposes that there never was a Zodiac killer at all, at least in the form of a single serial killer. Thomas Henry Horan authored the book, of the same name, where he presents his theory on the Zodiac murders. Horan creates a compelling case, showing evidence that points towards the idea that the Zodiac could never have been just one killer. He even states that the idea of a single Zodiac killer is purely a work of fiction. He points out the differences in weapons, ballistics, motives, and eyewitness accounts to drive his point home. He also discusses the likelihood that the letters were written by different authors. He believes that the only authentic "Zodiac" letters were the first three written and sent to the papers with the code as well as the follow-up letter. Horan also gives speculation as to who he believes actually committed the murders, although many of them have less weight than the actual Zodiac theory. In the documentary, other experts offer a rebuttal, explaining why they disagree with Horan's assumptions.

Horan does make some pretty stark accusations against Paul Avery, a reporter at the San Francisco Chronicle, saying that he believes that Avery wrote some of the letters and may have even broken into the police station to steal pieces of the bloody shirt to add to the letters he wrote. His only real evidence to support that theory is the fact that the Zodiac began sending his letters to only The Chronicle rather than the other media outlets he was using.

The other detectives and experts in the documentary do a great job of balancing the information and give the viewer a good overview of how Horan could be wrong in his theories. The handwriting experts on the show tackle the issue of the writing style changing after the Paul Stine murder. We also know that one of the detectives did write a few of the letters to entice the Zodiac to come out of hiding. So, it is definitely not implausible that some or all of the letters sent to the press and law enforcement could have been written by people who wanted to keep the fame going. However that doesn't mean that the five murders were committed by anyone other than the infamous Zodiac killer. There are several experts in the documentary that dismiss Horan's claims completely.

Final Thoughts - The Zodiac is a case that will probably never be solved and will remain a true crime hot-button for years to come. There will always be speculation as to who the Zodiac could be and why he committed these murders. The truth is, that after all these years he has done nothing but become a symbol of the unidentified killer that could be prowling our streets at any time. While it is a scary thought that someone could so callously kill, and just disappear, it is important that we are well aware of these possibilities, so we can keep ourselves and our loved ones as safe as possible. As many people have done before, it is up to us to investigate the evidence, take a look at the suspects, and come up with our own conclusions as to who this killer may have been.

Expand Your Mind

Podcasts
- *Murder Metal Mayhem* - Ep. 11 – "Zodiac-Palooza"
- *TimeSuck w/ Dan Cummins* - Bonus Ep. 12 – "The Zodiac Killer"
- *Last Podcast on the Left* - Eps. 83,84

Books
- *Zodiac Killer: Just the Facts* by Tom Voigt
- *The Most Dangerous Animal of All* by Gary L. Stewart

Documentaries
- *The Hunt for the Zodiac Killer* (2017)
- *The Most Dangerous Animal of All* (2020)
- *Myth of the Zodiac Killer* (2023)

CHAPTER SEVEN

JOHN WAYNE GACY

Gacy has been the subject of so much study over the last forty plus years since his capture. He is the epitome of the narcissistic power and control killer. Most people who knew him would never have believed what they found in his crawlspace. He was a successful business owner, who employed boys from all over the community. He was a member of the Democratic Party and even hosted Rosalynn Carter for a special dinner. He could be friendly, charming, and terrifying all at the same time. There have been movies,

TV shows, documentaries, and podcasts all done on the Killer Clown. John Borowski is currently finishing his epic miniseries called *The John Wayne Gacy Murders: Life and Death in Chicago*, scheduled for release in 2024. John has always been the most unbiased documentarian that I know; he includes all the facts and allows you to decide the truth for yourself. Bob Motta Jr., son of one of Gacy's defense attorneys, created the deep dive podcast *Defense Diaries*. In season one, he discusses the case and the tapes of Gacy interviews that his dad gave him, with reveals that are earth-shattering. Ryan Graveface owns the Graveface Museum, in Savannah, GA, and Chicago, IL, and owns the largest collection of Gacy murder-abilia ever amassed. He also has many other true crime artifacts including a room devoted to Ed Gein and a large collection of Heaven's Gate items. He also has events featuring some of the people directly related to these true crime events. Last year, there were several events featuring one of the members of Heaven's Gate. Gacy grew up very close to his two sisters and his mother. However, his father was an abusive alcoholic, who regularly beat him with a belt and called him names. When his mother would try to protect him from his father, he would call Gacy a "queer," "sissy," or "mamma's boy." In 1949, Gacy and another boy were caught fondling a girl and he was beaten severely because of it. There are several accounts of his father beating him unconscious. That same year, Gacy went to get ice cream with a family friend who would molest him instead. Some reports suggest that his father found out and threatened to call the police if that friend ever came around again. In other reports, it says that Gacy would never tell his father for fear that he would blame him.

As a child, Gacy was diagnosed with a heart condition and would experience blackouts. He was hospitalized for these conditions, but several accounts believe that it was because of the beatings from his father. In 1957, his appendix burst, and he had to have it removed. Through all of this, his father would believe that he was faking. He would always consider him a "weak" child and did not expect very much from him.

In 1962, Gacy moved to Las Vegas and worked as a mortuary assistant for 3 months. Gacy would later recount a strange story that occurred while working at this job. He felt compelled to get into a coffin with the body of a teenage boy and would cuddle and caress the body. This experience both excited and terrified him. Soon after this experience, he would quit the job and move back home. But this formative experience would start to shape him into the monster that he would become. Later, he would deny the claims that he had any sexual relations with the body of this teenage boy. However, if this story is true, it certainly places him in the realm of necrophilia. We often believe that necrophilia is only about having intercourse with a dead body, but there are actually ten classifications of necrophile. It seems that Gacy would fit Class Two: the romantic necrophile. They preserve the body and sleep with the body to gain a sense of comfort and possible sexual stimulation.

After being molested as a youth his second known homosexual experience would come in 1964 at a Jaycees event. The Jaycees are a non-profit organization that provides leadership training, business development, and community service to men between the ages of eighteen and forty years old. They have another division specifically for women of the same age range. Another member would get him drunk and ask him if he wanted to crash on his couch. That member would then perform oral sex on him while he was drunk. It is interesting that this experience parallelled the exact method Gacy would take later with many of his own victims. He often took his victims to discuss the possibility of a job and offered them alcohol to "loosen" them up.

Gacy married Marlynn Myers in 1964 and moved to Waterloo, Iowa to manage his father-in-law's KFC restaurants. During this time, he had a place in his basement where he would bring the young male staff, give them alcohol, and make sexual advances towards them. It was during this time that he perfected his handling of rejection. He would always claim to either be joking or testing them, if they denied his sexual advances. While he was the manager of KFC, he also took over the local chapter of the Jaycees. He became a great fundraiser, but he also became involved in drug abuse, pornography, prostitution, and wife-swapping.

In 1967, Gacy would run stag parties at the Jaycees events. Here he would continue to sexually assault young men. Donald Voorhees Jr. was invited back to Gacy's house, given alcohol, and persuaded to have mutual oral sex with Gacy. He would then sexually assault several more young men, even having one have sex with his wife and then blackmailing him to have oral sex with Gacy. But it was the sexual assault of Voorhees that would land him in jail after Donald told his father what happened. On May 10th, 1968, Gacy was indicted for sodomy. Gacy would then hire one of his employees to physically assault Voorhees, but Voorhees reported him and he also ended up in jail for his part in the conspiracy.

Gacy was evaluated during this time and determined to have an anti-social personality disorder. If only they had realized then the kind of monster Gacy would have become, they could have stopped him. On December 3rd, 1968, John Wayne Gacy was convicted and sentenced to ten years in prison. That day, his wife would also submit their divorce papers. While Gacy was in jail he was the model prisoner. He became the head cook in the kitchen, giving him lots of freedom in the prison. He joined the prison Jaycee chapter, was able to secure wage increases for inmates, and greatly improved conditions for the inmates at the prison. He would even get the prison to install a miniature golf course. Gacy was denied parole in 1969 but ultimately was released with twelve months of probation on June 18th, 1970, after serving only eighteen months of his sentence.

After his release he returned to Chicago and, per his probation, moved in with his mother. His parole ended on October 18th, 1971, but he was actually arrested twice during his probation and the reports were never relayed to Iowa. The first was on February 12th for sexually assaulting and luring a teenage boy into his car from a Greyhound station. The case would be dismissed because the teenager failed to appear in court. The second was on June 22nd when Gacy pretended to be a cop by flashing a badge at a youth before he lured him into his car and forced him to perform oral sex on Gacy. The charges in this case were dropped because the youth would attempt to blackmail Gacy.

In late 1971, Gacy and his mother moved into the infamous house at 8213 West Summerdale Avenue, where he would live until his arrest. He also started his own business in 1971 named, P.D.M. Contractors, which stood for Painting, Decorating, and Maintenance. This would be the business that he used to lure young men into working for him and often they would disappear. Gacy married Carole Hoff on July 1st, 1972, but by 1975 he would admit to her that he was bisexual and was no longer interested in having sex with her. During that time, he would often be absent, going out and not coming back until all hours of the night. She found homosexual pornography, and men's wallets, and observed Gacy bringing teenage boys into the garage at night. She eventually asked for a divorce in October 1975 but did not move out until February 1976.

His first known murder happened almost seven months before his second marriage. On January 3rd, 1972, he lured Timothy McCoy from the Greyhound bus station. He took him on a tour of Chicago ending at Gacy's house. He convinced McCoy to spend the night, but Gacy admitted he woke up in the morning to McCoy standing in his doorway with a knife. Gacy believed he was being attacked and wrestled the knife away from McCoy. He then stabbed him to death on the floor, having an orgasm in the process. As he was washing the knife, he realized that McCoy was only making him breakfast and had come to wake him up. He buried McCoy in the crawlspace and covered him in concrete. I could not find any information on where his mother was during this event. Gacy has admitted that the night before the murder there was a family party at his house. There is the possibility that his mother left with one of the relatives to visit, giving Gacy the freedom to commit the crime that he was longing to commit. His mother would often travel to Little Rock Arkansas to visit her daughter and it is a possibility that she took this time to make such a trip. It is recorded that just a few months later his mother moved out to allow him to get married to his second wife.

Gacy would have thirty-two more known victims, over the next six years. There were 26 victims buried in the crawlspace, three buried elsewhere on the property, and four thrown in the Des Plaines River. He rarely abducted anyone by force but preferred to talk them into going with him through offers of drugs and alcohol or by using a police badge to get them into the car. Once they were inside the home, he would get them both drunk and high to gain their trust and lower their inhibitions. He would then break out the handcuffs to show them the handcuff "trick." It was nothing more than him cuffing himself behind his back and producing a hidden cuff key to free himself. He would then talk them into putting on the cuffs so he could show them the "trick." This is when the monster would come out and his demeanor would completely change. He would then sexually abuse and torture the victims by burning them, drowning and reviving them, sodomizing them with various objects, as well as performing fellatio on them and forcing them to provide fellatio to him. The whole time he would make fun of them and degrade them before he would finish the job with his final "trick." Gacy would bring out the rope and tighten it around their throat in a tourniquet, strangling them as he watched them convulse, sometimes for hours.

Gacy was arrested on December 22nd, 1978, after the police found human remains in his crawlspace. After his final victim Robert Piest went missing, the police began tailing Gacy. They would eventually secure two search warrants. The first, on December 13th, allowed them into the house, where they would find several incriminating items. They found several police badges, handcuffs, hypodermic needles, books and films on homosexual pornography, several driver's licenses, underwear that was not his size, a blue hooded parka, and a ring with the initials J.A.S. December 21st, a second search warrant was issued, and this would be when they discovered the bodies in the crawlspace. Gacy would then make his first confession on December 22nd and the following day he would draw a map of all the bodies in the crawlspace.

On March 12th, 1978, Gacy was convicted on thirty-three charges of murder and sentenced to death thirty-three times, one death sentence for each murder. For the rest of his life, he would continue to work to overturn his conviction, claiming, "All the police are going to get me for is running a funeral parlor without a license." He would often attempt to prove that it was impossible for him to do any of the killing because his schedule was so busy. Gacy would even come up with a file, entitled "A Question of Doubt", including every piece of evidence that "proved" that he was innocent. This was later made into a book with the same title. Ultimately, he would be executed by lethal injection on May 9th, 1994, and his final words were reported to be, "Kiss my ass."

Myth #1: The House Smelled Bad Because of the Decaying Bodies

There has always been talk of the decaying body smell that Gacy's house emitted. In the Gacy episode of *Evil Lives Here*, Gacy's sister Karen recounts the musty, old smell she remembers the first time she entered her brother's new home. She also remembers a conversation with Gacy where he said that he should have cemented the crawlspace. There is also a prison interview where Gacy talks about the house always having a musty smell to it, especially when the dirt basement would get wet. In at least one of the movies about the Gacy story, you can see a puddle of putrefying flesh outside the house that Gacy is trying to cover up while his neighbors ask what the smell is. Is there any truth to this? How could you have twenty-six decaying corpses under your house without a nasty smell?

Gacy confessed to spreading quick lime in the crawlspace to both cover the smell and speed up the decomposition process. There is a popular story about Gacy's house where two investigators, Bob Schultz and Ron Robinson, were invited to dinner at Gacy's house before they served the second search warrant. While they were in the house one of the investigators used the restroom. As he was in the bathroom, the heating system kicked on and he could smell the decaying bodies in the crawlspace. During that same time frame, two of Gacy's employees were questioned and revealed that Gacy had them dig trenches in the crawlspace and that they spread lime in the crawlspace at Gacy's request. Later they would be asked where they thought Gacy might hide the body of Robert Piest, they would confirm that it must be in the crawlspace. So, which was it, did the detectives smell something or was it the information that they received from the employees that caused them to search the crawlspace? I had a conversation with retired Chicago detective William Dorsch, author of the book *Omnipotent: Don't Ask, Don't Tell*, about the claim of the smell. Bill knew Gacy and had even had dinner at his house; he would report that he never smelled anything. Bill, being an incredible detective, as well as having an encyclopedic knowledge of the case, gave me a rundown on the exact people involved and the date of the report. On December 23rd, 1978, there was a Des Plaines police report stating that Officer Robert Schultz told Lt. Kozenczak on the 21st that when Gacy invited him into his home two days prior, he immediately smelled and recognized a foul odor that he identified as putrefied flesh. He said that he first identified the smell when he entered the kitchen. It is interesting to note that he would wait two days to tell Lt. Kozenczak about the smell. Why didn't they talk about it that day? This was a man that they suspected of kidnapping and killing a young man, so why would this not have been important enough to report immediately? And then, why did it take an additional two days for the report to be filed?

When Gacy started killing and burying people in the crawlspace, his wife still lived in the home. She has only ever reported that sometimes she would smell a musty smell in the house, but it wasn't bad. John would also play it off, saying that it was a rat that died in the basement or some other animal. So, it seems that the combination of the graves dug, the quicklime, and the concrete was an effective way to cover up the smell of twenty-six decaying bodies. When Gacy knew that they had gotten the second search warrant. he would turn off the sump pump to flood the crawlspace, thinking that they would decide to not search that part of the home. This backfired completely because then the wet ground and the decaying bodies definitely caused a stench. However, before that, it seemed that there was little to no smell in the house or around it. It is fascinating to me that when Gacy was being tailed by the police, knowing that they were after him and may have been getting close, he would allow them into his home at all. He seems to have had very little fear of getting caught or was narcissistic enough to believe that he could charm them into giving up on their search.

Myth #2: Gacy Killed People While Dressed as Pogo the Clown

John Wayne Gacy will forever be known as the Killer Clown. Although I am sure that people have been afraid of clowns since they have been around, the modern fear of clowns and their influence in the movies have all originated from the story of Gacy and Pogo the Clown. The idea of the creepy clown lurking in the shadows is no more terrifying than in the stories of the Stephen King novel and movies, *It*. Oddly enough, this is also my favorite novel of all time, I have read it over a hundred times and still love it. It has always been debated if King's original inspiration was Gacy, himself. In a few articles and interviews, King would deny that he took the idea of Pennywise from the account of Gacy. However, the idea of a clown that kills children seems closely related to the story of Gacy. Even if inspiration came from Pogo the Clown, does that mean that Gacy used that persona to kill?

This myth has been around for years but happened to be dramatized at the end of the Netflix *Dahmer* show. We see a scene of Gacy dressed as Pogo the Clown drowning a man in the bathtub. All of this is actually taken from Gacy's own confessions. He admitted to drowning victims only to then revive them as a form of torture, however, he was adamant that he never killed anyone dressed as Pogo the Clown. It seems that his clowning was actually his safe space. It was the one place where he could feel normal and not be the monster. To me, this is fascinating. Most people put on masks or wear a costume to disassociate from their crimes, becoming another person, so they don't have to really deal with the horrors they commit. Or it allows them to fully immerse themselves in their own fantasy life. This was not the case with Gacy, who would use the clown persona to dive into his humanity. It was the only time that he could interact with people in a childlike state; the rest of the time he was looking to scheme and position people where he could get what he wanted.

Gacy had a very specific fantasy and it all had to do with having power and control over his victims. Gacy enjoyed sweet-talking his victims and getting them into a vulnerable place. He needed to lull them into a false sense of security and would often get them to willingly engage in sexual acts with him. He needed the thrill of "tricking" them into a compromising position, so he could finally let out the monster that he kept hidden within. Then it was too late, for most of them, when the monster took control, he would torture them physically, mentally, and sexually for hours to fulfill that dark fantasy before he killed them. His fantasy would then go even further; he kept mementos of his victims and even needed to keep them physically with him. Many killers will take the bodies and dump them at locations where they can go visit and continue the fantasy. Gacy kept the majority of them under his house where he never had to be without them. It wasn't until the space became too full that he started to dump the bodies in the river. With all that being said, it could never fit Gacy's fantasy of power and control to do that as Pogo or Patches the Clown, that was his method of giving back to the community.

Myth #3: Gacy Was in Possession of the Robert Piest Receipt

If you watch any documentary about the life and crimes of John Wayne Gacy the one thing they all reference is a receipt that was found in the trash. The receipt in question was signed by Kim Byers, who worked with Robert Piest. She reported to the police that she had a roll of film to develop; she placed it in the envelope, signed the receipt, and placed the receipt in the pocket of Robert Piest's blue parka. Later in some interviews, she mentioned that she initially wadded up the receipt and threw it in the trash, but then felt compelled to take it out and keep it. Is it true, just because every documentary says it is? My friend and son of one of Gacy's defense attorneys, Bob Motta Jr., would be the person to break the story of an alternate theory of the Robert Piest receipt.

In season one of *Defense Diaries: The Gacy Tapes,* a podcast by Bob Motta Jr., we learn that the second search warrant was predicated on the finding of the receipt that was, supposedly, placed in the pocket of Robert Piest's parka. A coworker of Robert had been wearing his jacket at work that day and said that she had placed the photo receipt in the pocket. It has always been believed that it was then found in the trash at Gacy's house. Here is where the story gets interesting. As the police were surveilling Gacy and his property, it is believed that Gacy put out the trash, they took the bag and found the receipt in it. However, this piece of critical evidence doesn't appear on the chain of custody evidence list, until much later. When Bob interviewed several of the police involved, he confirmed that they never found the trash outside of Gacy's house. They happened to stop the garbage truck after they picked up Gacy's trash and this bag was obtained from inside the back of the truck, which means it could have been from any place on that truck's route. The bag was also not examined on the scene but transported to the lab, where sometime later the receipt was "found."

What does this mean to us? It doesn't change the fact that Gacy was a horrible monster and killed at least thirty-three young men. However, it does bring up the real possibility that police misconduct could have been at play. In our country, there are countless cases of people being wrongfully imprisoned. This all starts with bias in law enforcement, which can come in many forms, cultural, ethnic, or religious being just a few. Many of these cases include some form of police misconduct, ranging from planting evidence to quick arrests made under the pressure to convict someone so the community is satisfied. The public often wants its bloodlust satiated, reminding me of imagery from the Roman Colosseum where the spectators were entertained with poor souls fighting for their lives in the arena. In Gacy's case, the receipt could have been planted so that they could obtain the second search warrant, where they found the twenty-six bodies in the crawlspace. However, what if that happened to you or me? Police misconduct becomes a slippery slope and is an abuse of power that could potentially put the rights of innocent people at risk. If nothing else, it makes us question our trust in the police and should compel us to put better safeguards in place to keep our law enforcement accountable for their actions.

Legend: Gacy Killed More Than the 33 Known Victims

There has always been speculation that Gacy killed many more than the thirty-three believed victims. He had been honing his own personal skill set of killing for years. We know that when Gacy lived in Waterloo, Iowa he was already engaging in deviant behaviors. He had a basement where he would throw parties with the young male employees from the KFC locations he managed. We also know that he would make sexual advances toward them. This is also where he began his time with the Jaycees and would have all the "stag" parties, where they would watch both straight and gay pornography. This would eventually lead him to his first prison stay for the assault of Donald Voorhees. The question has always been, did his killing really start once he made it to 8213 Summerdale Ave, or had it already begun long before?

When Gacy was originally arrested, he claimed to have killed up to forty-five people, but only thirty-three have been officially attributed to Gacy. Sadly, there are still five of those victims who remain unidentified. If his original estimation was true, where are those bodies located? There has been speculation about the home in Waterloo, his mother's home, and several other locations where PDM Contractors was working. One of the specific places they believed Gacy dumped bodies was a wall that was bricked up at the Ranibo Roller Rink that they helped build. There were human remains and clothing that were found there later, but it has never been officially attributed to Gacy. It is really strange to me that they find two bodies in a place where a known serial killer worked, and they don't even attempt to investigate it in connection to the Gacy murders. Is this just because the city wanted all the talk about Gacy to be over? Or are there other reasons that the city has never wanted to investigate the potential of other victims?

Retired Chicago Detective William Dorsch believes that Gacy was burying bodies at an apartment building that he maintained at West Miami Ave. He personally saw Gacy with a shovel there, digging trenches in the night. This property was searched twice, once in 1998 and again in 2013. They used ground penetrating radar, which proved that there were at least fourteen anomalies suggesting possible human remains. They would dig in a few spots, where they were told nothing was displayed on the radar before they closed the case. It is baffling to understand how they could close the case until you look at the media circus around these murders. The Chicago Police Department did not want any more bodies to be found because it would force them to reopen this case, proving the ineptitude of law enforcement and implicating many people who had built their careers on this case. Currently, the powerhouse team of Bob Motta Jr. and William Dorsch have teamed up to investigate some of these locations and to find out the truth. There are several interviews that Bill has done that show the police actively discounting witness statements and not following up with witnesses to keep this case closed. So, did Gacy have more victims? Are there more bodies out there that need to be found? Can more families be given closure, by providing some answer to their missing children? This will all be part of *The Gacy Tapes* Season Two and I cannot wait to see what they find. Secretly, I am hoping that I get the phone call and I get to dig some of the holes myself.

We may never truly know when the killing spree of John Wayne Gacy began, although there is a ton of evidence that it either began before the murder of Timothy McCoy in 1972 or that there were many more in the three years until he murdered John Butkovich in 1975. What I do know is that the duo of Motta and Dorsch are on the case and if there is anything to find they will find it. As Bob Motta likes to say, "Get the straight dope and just the facts" by tuning in to *Defense Diaries*. I will certainly be there lurking in the chat, listening for each sordid detail as it gets uncovered.

Expand Your Mind

Podcasts

- *Murder Metal Mayhem* - Ep. 87 – "John Wayne Gacy: In the Crawlspace"
- *Defense Diaries* Podcast Season 1: "The Gacy Tapes" & Season 2: "The Search for Additional Victims"
- *TimeSuck w/ Dan Cummins* - Ep. 68 – "John Wayne Gacy: Chicago's Serial Killing Clown"
- *Last Podcast on the Left* - Eps. 105, 106

Books

- *John Wayne Gacy: Hunting a Predator* by John Borowski
- *Killer Clown: The John Wayne Gacy Murders* by Terry Sullivan
- *The Last Victim* by Jason Moss

Documentaries & Movies

- *Conversations with a Killer: The John Wayne Gacy Tapes* (2022)
- *John Wayne Gacy: Devil in Disguise* (2021)
- *Dear Mr. Gacy* (2010)

CHAPTER EIGHT

TED BUNDY

If there is one case that will be forever etched into the annals of true crime history, it is the case of Ted Bundy. There have been many cases before him and since, but none showed us the horrors of what a smiling face, an intelligent mind, and the depravity of a soul could do within our society. The case of Ted Bundy had far reaching implications for our law enforcement, investigations, and psychology. We finally got a real look inside the mind of a killer. Sadly, it would only be the beginning.

Ted Bundy's birthname was Theodore Robert Cowell, born on November 24th, 1946, in Burlington Vermont. When Ted would describe his childhood, he often said that it was just a typical childhood, with nothing that would give you any indication of what he would become. Although this is almost certainly not true, he would always say this in his prison interviews. By 1950 Ted and his mother moved from Philadelphia to Washington. A year later, she met Johnny Bundy, and eventually, he would adopt Ted, giving him the last name that would become infamous.

In 1967, while attending the University of Washington, he met Diane Edwards and they began a romantic relationship. Later, Ted would say that she was the only woman he ever loved. Bundy dropped out of college in 1968 and volunteered for positions within the Republican Party. He even ended up earning a scholarship to Stanford University. Sadly, shortly after all that transpired, Diane broke up with him, saying he had no ambition and was immature.

By the end of 1969, Bundy was back in Washington and started dating a single mother named Elizabeth Kloepfer. They had an abusive relationship that would continue until after he was arrested for the first time in 1976. Later, Bundy would be accused of molesting her daughter when she was around age seven.

Bundy graduated from the University of Washington in 1972 and was accepted into two law schools. In 1973, he reignited a relationship with Diane Edwards, while he was still dating Elizabeth Kloepfer. He would even begin talking about marriage with Edwards, even introducing her as his fiancée. In early 1974, he disappeared and broke off all contact with Edwards. Later, she would believe that he only wanted to get her to fall in love with him, so he could break it off and hurt her the same way she had hurt him. Just a few short months later, he stopped attending law school altogether.

We will never know when Bundy began killing. There are people that believe that he started in his teens and others who believe he started in 1969, just after Edwards broke up with him. This is one of the reasons why no one has an accurate number of victims for Ted Bundy. He would also tell different people different stories, so it is hard to know what the truth actually is.

The officially accepted crimes began in 1974, just as he cut off his relationship with Edwards. He began killing in the states of Washington and Oregon, leaving eight women in his wake. There were several eyewitnesses who would give descriptions of a man, either wearing a sling or on crutches, attempting to lure women by asking for help. This would become Bundy's modus operandi; he would disarm these women by playing the wounded victim. Once they agreed to help him and lowered their defenses, the beast would come out and attack them. He would then take them to a remote location, rape them, and kill them. There were times that he went back to his dump sites to rape the bodies he had dumped there. He was reported as a potential suspect by several people close to him, but the police ignored it believing that a law student with no criminal background couldn't possibly commit these crimes.

Bundy then moved to Utah to attend law school for the second time in August of 1974. During his time there he killed nine women in three additional states: Idaho, Utah, and Colorado. When he committed his crimes in 1974, he kept several of the women captive for extended periods of time. One of his victims, the medical examiner estimated, was held for up to twenty days before he murdered her. During that time, he would rape and torture them. After they were dead, he would continue returning to the scene to defile the bodies. Although, the typical M.O. of Ted Bundy was to kidnap, rape, strangle, and dump the bodies of his victims, usually within the same day. This year seems to have been a year of evolution in his killing, by medical examiners' accounts.

One year later, Bundy was arrested in Utah. An officer would see a Volkswagen Beetle in a residential area, early in the morning. Upon seeing the officer, Bundy fled and the officer followed in a high-speed chase. Eventually, the officer got Bundy to pull over, and searched the car. He found a ski mask, a pantyhose mask, handcuffs, rope, trash bags, a crowbar, an ice pick, and burglary tools. They would also later search his apartment, and found several guides and brochures with locations marked, which corresponded with some of the abduction locations. They missed the polaroids that he would take of his victims, though. After they released him, on lack of evidence, he would go home and destroy the photographs.

In September 1975, Bundy sold his Volkswagen Beetle, and the police impounded and searched the vehicle. They found hairs linking him to three of the known victims. On October 2nd, Bundy was placed in a lineup and positively identified by Carol DaRonch, who escaped from Bundy after he tried to abduct her by posing as a police officer. He was charged with aggravated kidnapping and attempted assault but was released on a $15,000 bond. His parents paid the bond and Bundy was released. The police would continue their surveillance and intensify the pressure on Bundy.

Although the police were certain that Bundy was the culprit, they had little hard evidence to charge him with. He stood trial for the kidnapping of Carol DaRonch in February 1976 and was sentenced to one to fifteen years in the Utah State Prison. Four months into serving his sentence, his first escape attempt would be foiled. Bundy would be found in possession of maps, an airline schedule, and a new social security card. He spent a few weeks in solitary as punishment for his escape attempt. Shortly after this event, he was charged with his first murder, and in early 1977 he was transferred to Aspen, Colorado.

He would eventually end up at the Pitkin County Courthouse in Aspen for a preliminary trial. In this trial, he elected to act as his own counsel and during a recess he asked to use the law library. While in the library, he would jump from the second-story window and was on the run for six days before the police caught him. During that time, he broke into several cabins to steal the needed food and supplies. He got lost on the mountain for a few days, before finally, he stole a car and was caught a short time later.

Bundy was placed back in the Garfield County Jail, and he immediately began his plans for another escape. It is believed that he may have had a good chance of beating the murder charge, but all that went out the window with his second successful escape. Bundy would get his hands on a detailed floor plan of the jail and a hacksaw blade and used the blade to saw a one-square-foot hole in the ceiling. During that time, he was also starving himself to lose the weight that he needed to fit through the hole for the escape. On December 30th, 1977, Bundy made his escape. He went through the hole in his ceiling, broke through the ceiling of the chief jailer, stole his clothes, and walked out the front door. The jail wouldn't discover the missing inmate until nearly 24 hours later, and by that time, Bundy had already made it to Chicago.

Just nine days later, on January 8th, 1978, Bundy arrived in Tallahassee, Florida. One week later, Bundy committed the Chi Omega Murders. He entered the sorority house around 2:45 a.m. and assaulted four women, killing two in the process. The four attacks would be determined to take less than fifteen minutes and did not disturb any of the thirty or so other people sleeping in the same house. Just eight blocks away, he broke into another apartment and attacked another woman, leaving her for dead.

On February 8th, 1978, Bundy attempted to abduct a fourteen-year-old girl in Jacksonville Florida. However, her older brother confronted him, and Bundy ran away. Sadly, he was undeterred, and the next day he kidnapped his last victim from Lake City Middle School. She was a twelve-year-old girl that Bundy brutally raped and murdered, before dumping her body 40 miles northwest of Lake City near Suwannee State Park.

Bundy continued to steal cars, traveling west. On February 15th, 1978, in the early morning, Bundy was stopped by an officer. The officer would realize that the car he was driving was stolen, and Bundy would try to escape but the officer chased him down and tackled him. There would be a brief fight over the officer's gun, but he ultimately subdued Bundy. The officer wouldn't know for some time that he had just arrested someone on the FBI's Most Wanted list.

Bundy faced trial for the Chi Omega murders in June 1979. He was convicted of both murders, three counts of attempted murder, and two counts of burglary. During the trial, he would provide his own defense, but he would still end up with two death sentences. In December 1979, Bundy would again face the courts for the kidnapping and murder of Kimberley Leach. He would, again, provide his own defense, and this time he would use his time in court to marry Carole Ann Boone. He actually met Carole in 1974, while they worked together in the Department of Emergency Services in Olympia, Washington. Bundy wanted to date her, but for six years they only had a platonic relationship. However, during that time Ted would constantly use Carole for support and weave a web that would entangle her until she became his wife and the mother of his child. Ultimately, Bundy would receive his third death sentence on February 10th, 1980. Just over two years later, in October 1982, Carole Ann Boone gave birth to a daughter, Rosa Bundy.

After his final sentencing, almost nine years went by before the execution was carried out. During that time, Bundy would work his way through the appeal process, always hoping that his sentence would be overturned. He also did a series of police interviews with varying levels of admission. It would also not be the end of his escape attempts. In July of 1984, they tossed Bundy's cell to find several hacksaw blades in his possession and a section of the cell window completely through and glued back into place. After Bundy was discovered, he continued to find ways to be relevant, even offering his services in "psychology" to help catch the Green River Killer.

In April 1986, Bundy finally confessed to what would be believed to be the entirety of his crimes to Hagmaier and Nelson. On the road to January 24th, 1989, when Bundy finally faced the electric chair, there would be several stays of execution and rescheduling. But ultimately all the shirts and chants would come true, "Burn Bundy Burn."

Myth #1: Ted Had a Good Childhood

Bundy would always claim that he had a perfectly ordinary childhood, and even had childhood friends who would substantiate those claims. However, with a little further digging, you will find that his childhood was far from normal. It seems that it would begin at his birth with the sheer fact that he was an illegitimate child. His mother Louise Cowell, who Bundy believed was his sister most of his childhood, would never tell anyone who his father was, although she knew. There were several theories on who the father was, from a war veteran to a salesman, although it would never be confirmed. There was also a belief that it was his grandfather, Samuel Cowell, who molested his daughter, and therefore, Ted Bundy was a product of incest. We will never truly know, but from what we now know about genetics it could have been helpful in really determining what made up Ted.

It seems from all accounts that Ted was close to his grandfather during his time living in Philadelphia. However, his grandfather had an explosive temper, could become very violent, and experienced hallucinations. He abused everyone in the household, likely including Ted, as well as the animals. The young Ted would witness all of this at a very young age. At three years old, he started exhibiting some strange behavior. His aunt would wake up in her bed surrounded by knives, with a smiling Ted looming nearby.

In the early 1950s, Ted and his mother moved across the country, ending up in Tacoma, Washington. This was where

Ted would grow up, meet several new "fathers", and finally be adopted to receive his infamous surname. As a child, Ted had a speech impediment and was often made fun of by the other children. He also struggled to keep up with the other students because he was only a fair athlete and did not excel academically. When he was in the Boy Scouts, there was an account of him hitting another child in the head with a stick from behind. He was known to enjoy scaring people. He would also play a game where he would dig holes, place stakes into the bottom of the hole, and cover the hole with leaves and sticks hoping someone would fall in and get impaled. One girl eventually fell in and was injured by his trap. There were also stories of Ted abusing animals. It is said that he would trap mice and rip them apart. In an interview in 2016, one of Bundy's attorneys told a story of Ted buying mice from a pet store and using them to "play God." He would select which ones would live or die, forming the ultimate idea of control in his young mind.

As Ted moved into his teenage years, he became interested in pulp detective and porn magazines that he claimed he found in trash cans around the neighborhood. In later, interviews he would blame all his crimes on these early influences of porn. This idea borders on the ridiculous, but it would certainly shape his mind as an adolescent. There are accounts of Ted going into the closets at his junior high to masturbate. The other children caught him masturbating on several occasions and would throw water on him. I am certain that this type of ridicule would have a profound effect on him and his anti-social personality.

Around the age of thirteen, Ted became a "peeping Tom", peeking into his neighbor's windows and masturbating in the bushes. This was the first form of early escalation in what would become increasingly alarming sexual behaviors, transforming him into the sexual sadist that he would become in his adult years. It is commonly believed that Ted's killing spree started in 1974, but my good friend and Bundyphile,

E.J. Hammon believes that Ted may have started as early as fourteen years old. A few miles away from the home where Bundy lived in Tacoma, an eight-year-old girl, Ann Marie Burr was abducted from her home on August 31st, 1961, and would never be found. During that time, Bundy had a paper route, and this house was close to his route. Although Bundy denied having anything to do with the disappearance of Ann, it is completely conceivable that while he was out peeping, he could no longer control his desires and saw her as easy prey. Just before his execution, he made some allusions that could indicate that he did in fact kidnap and kill this child.

So, for all the talk that Ted has done and stories that he has told about his idyllic upbringing, you can see the truth does not support that narrative. He was a child who was exposed to abuse, sexual misconduct, possible incest, and all sorts of trauma. The narcissism that he exhibited at an early age and his evolving sexual depravity would culminate into unimaginable depths in adulthood. Our childhood is our most formative years. We will struggle with the trauma that we face early on for most of our lives unless we deal with it. Ted would become the perfect storm of intelligence, narcissism, and violence, using all the tools from psychology to support the depraved desires that he held within.

Myth #2: Ted Spared His Former Girlfriends

Ted Bundy would only have three real relationships with women his entire life. You would think that he would have been close to his mother, Louise, but since he believed she was his sister during most of his childhood, he never had a chance to form a real bond with his mother. In fact, she would initially leave him where he was born, at a home for unwed mothers in Burlington, Vermont intending to move on with her life. However, three months later she came back to pick him up. His mother considered putting him up for adoption but was dissuaded by her father. This would lead to Ted being told that his mother was his older sister. Ted and his mother would never have a close relationship.

Ted's first real relationship with a woman was in 1967 when he met Diane Edwards. Ted would later say that she was the only woman that he ever truly loved. Her family was wealthy and expected much of Diane and whoever would become her significant other. Initially, things went very well in their relationship, and Ted seemed like he was very ambitious and going places. However, when Ted dropped out of school, Diane decided that they were on different paths and broke up with him. This would be a defining moment in Ted's life and, if you believe the common story, Ted would immediately start killing for the first time. He would certainly kill in his anger and anguish, after what he would see as an inconceivable betrayal.

In 1969, Ted would meet Liz Kloepfer and start dating her. Liz stayed with Ted until midway through his first kidnapping trial and still supported him during that time, "hoping" that he was innocent. Liz was a single mother who was recently divorced. She was struggling with many of her own issues and Ted compounded that. They had a very difficult six-year relationship where Ted was constantly absent. During his moments of absence, he would either be killing or cheating. She was unaware of the cheating until after their relationship was already over. During the time they were dating, [?] Liz would talk to the police on at least three occasions. She turned Ted in, suspecting that he was the killer that they were looking for. Ted would cheat on Liz during this time with Diane Edwards and would even get Diane to agree to marry him. In typical narcissistic fashion, this was all to pay her back for betraying him, and he would immediately break it off with Diane. At one point, Ted also proposed to Liz, and she said yes. Later on, Ted would get mad at Liz and tear up the marriage license in her face. It seems that it would just be a measure of control to remind her that he could do whatever he wanted. Later Ted would admit that he had tried to kill her and her daughter but stopped himself. Was this because of love or was it some form of self-preservation? He must have known that killing someone so close to him would definitely get him caught. Ted likely never had any regard for women no matter how close he was to them.

The final woman in Ted's life was Carole Boone. He met her while dating Liz and would have a brief relationship with her. After he was convicted for the kidnapping of Carole DaRonch in 1976, Liz left him and Ted would be on the lookout for a new person to manipulate. While he was on trial for the Chi Omega murders in 1978, he reconnected with Carole. He found someone who would believe in his innocence, and she would even move to Florida to be closer to Ted. Ted put her on the stand as a character witness, finding a loophole to marry her in the process. Although there was "no contact" with the prisoners, somehow Carole would become pregnant with Ted's daughter. She continued a relationship with Ted until 1986, just three years before his execution.

The belief that Ted spared any of these women, is just a fallacy. He may not have killed them like he killed so many other women, but he certainly manipulated and destroyed them psychologically. He would use them to support the two lives that he was living and give him the feeling of "normality" that he needed to mask his darker desires of the night. The only reason Ted would spare any of these women is because he knew that it was too close to home. He was an intelligent killer, who only murdered people with whom he had little to no connection. He knew the risks of murdering people that the police could tie to you, so he never did. However, he was a terrible partner and used any manipulation that he could to keep his relationships going. He was a true narcissist, who believed he was never wrong in anything that he ever did. In the few moments where he did acknowledge any wrongdoing, he would manipulate the situation to place the blame on someone else. When Ted would apologize or feel sorry for something it would always be a means to lower their defenses so he could get another foothold in. Although he didn't kill them, he would leave each of them with undeniable scars that they would deal with the rest of their lives.

Myth #3: Ted Wanted to Get Caught

There is a prevailing thought in psychology that criminals want to get caught. The theory is that they feel, often subconsciously, guilt and remorse for their crimes and make mistakes that get them caught. The key point there is guilt and remorse. The one thing that we know about psychopaths is that they do not feel guilt or remorse. Bundy was a true psychopath and could barely pretend to have empathy for others. Like a true predator, he would learn how to fake or mask emotion to lure people into his trap. Every single emotion or tear that he would shed would be another attempt to get what he wanted, a ploy to work out his master plan, or some insidious way to complete his devious goals.

Bundy would do everything in his power to control the room, and thus he could not have anyone else represent him in a court of law. His extreme narcissism would never allow him to take a backseat to anyone. In doing so, he would completely destroy his chances for anything but the death penalty for his crimes. While most serial killers will allow their lawyers to plead their case, many of them will take a plea deal or confess to lessen their sentence. Bundy was unable to admit any guilt and thus sealed his own fate.

The third, possibly most obvious, evidence of the fact that Bundy did not want to be caught was that he escaped twice. The truth is Bundy not only escaped by jumping out the second-story window and starving himself to get out of his cell, in two of the most famous escapes. He also knocked down and ran from the officer who would ultimately arrest him for the final time. In 1984, just five years before his execution, Bundy was caught with hacksaw blades and the bars of his cell had been sawed through. Obviously, Bundy had no intention of spending the rest of his life in jail. Thankfully, he would never get the opportunity to escape again, but he tried everything he could to stave off his execution. All of the interviews, the confessions, and the help with other serial killer cases were part of Bundy's plan to avoid death. I have no doubt that he would have never stopped trying to escape if he had avoided the death penalty. Although Bundy loved the media attention, which fed his narcissistic personality, he was compelled to kill by force, which is foreign to most of us. If nothing else, the murders in Florida prove that Bundy was unable to control his need to cause terror and feed the beast that lived within him.

Legend: Ted Picked Up Debbie Harry in NYC

My friend E.J. Hammon, the Bundyphile and co-author of *Ted Bundy: Memories of the Beast,* brought this incredible story to my attention. After the execution of Ted Bundy in 1989, Debbie Harry would claim that she escaped an abduction by Bundy in 1972. She claims that in the early morning, she was looking for a cab on the Lower East Side of New York City. She had been walking for a little while, unable to find a cab, and noticed a white VW Beetle following her. The driver told her that he would take her to any destination she wanted. Ultimately, she would take him up on his offer and get into the car, only to quickly realize that it was a mistake when she noticed there were no door handles on the inside of the car. By that time, it was too late, the door was shut, and they were on the move. Thankfully, the window was cracked just enough to let air flow into the car where she could get her hand into the crack. She would pull the window down enough to reach the handle on the outside, and when they took a sharp turn, she opened the car door and fell out of the car. In a providential turn of events, the driver would continue to drive away.

In her excellent article on bundyphile.com, E.J. points out some inconsistencies in Debbie's story. The first is the location. Bundy was never known to be in the New York area in 1972. This would happen to be the exact time that Bundy was working on the Suicide Hotline with Ann Rule. He was also working on the reelection campaign of Republican Governor Dan Evans, so it seems very unlikely that Bundy would be taking a cross-country trip to New York to abduct a hapless victim.

The second is her description of the car. We know that the VW Beetles that Bundy used were either tan or beige, but not white. One of the VW Beetles used by Ted Bundy is on display at Alcatraz East Crime Museum in Pigeon Forge, Tennessee. If you take a close look at that vehicle, you will see that the interior of the VW is normal; Bundy had not removed any of the interior hardware. Honestly, he didn't need to. Most of the women that he abducted were knocked out before they ever entered the vehicle.

Finally, E.J. mentions the time frame in which Debbie Harry "remembers" her abductor. It would be seventeen years after the experience that she would finally realize that it was, in fact, Ted Bundy who had abducted her. By that time, Bundy had been national news for the last eleven years, but she would just now, since his death, notice his face in the paper. She may have had a terrible experience, but it was certainly not Ted Bundy who did it.

Podcasts

- *TimeSuck w/ Dan Cummins* - Ep. 11 – "Ted Bundy: Real Life Monster"
- *Last Podcast on the Left* - Eps. 99, 100

Books

- *Ted Bundy: Memories of the Beast* by E.J. Hammon & Fabian Richards
- *The Stranger Beside Me* by Ann Rule
- *The Bundy Murders* by Kevin M. Sullivan
- *The Enigma of Ted Bundy* by Kevin Sullivan

Documentaries & Movies

- *Conversations with a Killer: The Ted Bundy Tapes* (2019)
- *Ted Bundy: Mind of a Monster* (2019)
- *Extremely Wicked, Shockingly Evil and Vile* (2019)
- *No Man of God* (2021)
- Ted Bundy Interviews - YouTube

CHAPTER NINE

JEFFREY DAHMER

The story of Jeffrey Dahmer has become a gripping tale. He is both a tragic figure and a brutal cannibal who scoured the red-light district of Milwaukee, Wisconsin looking for victims. The recent Netflix *Dahmer* series, with its creative liberties, showed the complicated figure that Dahmer was. It is rare that we see someone who is so lost in their own psychosis that they create an altar of bones, yet continue to go to work and associate with other people. Unlike other killers that we have described, Dahmer was not trying to hide his crimes in any conventional sense. He did not try to find random victims, he did not attempt to clean up the crime scene, and he did not try to hide the bodies. He would kill as if in a trance, a drunken trance. In this state, he killed at least seventeen men from 1978 to 1991.

On May 21st, 1960, Jeffrey Dahmer was born in Milwaukee, Wisconsin. His father, Lionel Dahmer, was busy with school and then work for most of his childhood. His mother, Joyce Dahmer, was a hypochondriac and suffered from severe depression most of her life. So, from an early age, Jeffrey was often left to his own devices and largely ignored by his parents. Later, Jeffrey would recount the numerous arguments between his parents, during his childhood. He would never find a sense of stability in their family.

Jeffrey seemed to be a "normal" child up until he had a double hernia surgery just before he turned four years old. Lionel Dahmer, in his book *A Father's Story*, would recount that after the surgery Jeffrey was in so much pain, he believed that they cut off his penis. After the surgery, it seemed he was never the same. He went from a normal, happy, energetic child to a quiet, morose, distant child. Lionel wondered if this was when Jeffrey began to have all the dark thoughts. Just a short time after the surgery, they found a dead animal under the house. Lionel would remember how excited Jeffrey was at the sound that the bones made, calling them "fiddlesticks." This was the first time that Jeffrey was known to be interested in dead things, but it would become a life-long passion of his. Later, his father would teach him taxidermy, in an effort to try and connect with his son.

In October 1966, Lionel and Joyce had a second son and Jeffrey was given the honor of naming his baby brother. He would name his brother David. They would only be six years apart in age, but in reality, they couldn't be more different. This was also the year that Lionel graduated from college and began working as a chemist in Akron, Ohio.

Just two years later in 1968, they moved the family to a house in Bath, Ohio. Now that Jeffrey was eight years old and had some land that he could wander on, he began collecting and storing skeletons of dead animals. He learned how to preserve them in formaldehyde so that he could keep them and look at them. A few years later, Lionel taught him how to safely bleach the bones to further preserve them. At this point, Jeffrey began picking up larger animals and roadkill to dissect and bury. He would become fascinated by what was inside the animal's body and how the body worked.

Jeffrey attended Revere High School in Ohio, and although he was only a freshman, he had already begun drinking heavily, inside and outside of school. Although he was drinking in class, he was still intelligent with average grades. The other students didn't seem to like him very much, but the teachers thought he was polite and well-mannered. It was during this time that Jeffrey started to go through puberty, and he realized that he was attracted to other men. He began exploring these desires with another teenage boy, but it would only last a short time. Dahmer would later admit that he was already fantasizing about dominating and controlling a submissive male, and he would masturbate fantasizing about the male chest and torso.

When Jeffrey was sixteen, he would become sexually attracted to a male jogger that he saw in the neighborhood. He would fantasize about knocking the male unconscious and having his way with his body. He would watch him day after day, gathering the courage to confront him. Then one day, Dahmer hid in the bushes with a baseball bat lying in wait for the jogger. Thankfully that day the jogger would not run by. However, this was the first time that Dahmer would attempt to act on his darker impulses regarding another human being.

Jeffrey's drinking continued to get out of hand, and by 1977 his grades were beginning to decline. This was also the year that Lionel would discover that Joyce had an affair. They started the divorce proceedings and Lionel moved out of the house in early 1978. In May, Jeffrey graduated high school, and almost immediately after, his mother moved out with his brother, leaving Jeffrey to fend for himself in the family home, at only eighteen years old. The divorce was final on July 24th, 1978.

With Jeffrey alone in the house, with no supervision, he would be free to live out his darkest desires. Just three weeks after his graduation, Jeffrey murdered his first victim. Dahmer would lure Steven Mark Hicks to his home offering him some beers. Hicks was on his way to a concert at Chippewa Lake, and in typical fashion for the late 70s was hitchhiking to get there. Dahmer saw him standing on the side of the road with no shirt on and was immediately sexually attracted to Hicks. He picked him up and brought him to the house, but Hicks continued to talk about all the girls he was going to meet, and Dahmer knew that he would not be interested in him. They would drink and listen to music for several hours before finally Hicks asked Dahmer to take him to the lake for the concert. This would become the M.O. for all of Dahmer's murders; his extreme reaction to abandonment would show itself for the first time here. He would hit Hicks twice from behind with a ten-pound barbell. When he fell, he strangled him to death with the barbell, masturbated over the body, and then dismembered him in the basement. At first, he would bury him in a shallow grave in the backyard, but several weeks later he dug him up and then used the methods taught to him by his father to strip the flesh from the bones, crushing the bones with a sledgehammer, and scattering them around the woods of the property. This would be one of the rare times that we saw Dahmer take more traditional steps to cover up the crime so no one could find the body. It would be nine years until

Dahmer would kill again, but once he got started, he would be unable to stop.

Six weeks would go by after the murder of Steven Hicks before Lionel Dahmer would visit the house to find Jeffrey living there by himself and that his mother had abandoned him. His father forced him to be productive and enroll at Ohio State University. Jeffrey would only spend one semester at OSU, before dropping out. His drinking was completely out of hand, and he was failing just about every class that he had. After he dropped out, his father would tell him that if he couldn't hack it in college, he needed some discipline and would urge him to join the military. By January of 1979, Jeffrey began Army boot camp at Fort McClellan in Anniston, Alabama. He would end up training as a medical specialist and be stationed at Fort Sam Houston in Houston, Texas. Throughout his time in the military, he was disciplined for his drinking habits; regardless of the structure, he was almost constantly drunk.

In a strange turn of events, Dahmer was deployed to Baumholder, West Germany on July 13th, 1979, and served as a combat medic. During his first year, he would be considered an above-average soldier. Sadly, this would not continue, as his alcoholism would get the better of him. He received an honorable discharge from the military in March 1981. He would then fly to Fort Jackson in South Carolina to receive his debriefing and a plane ticket to anywhere in the country. Jeffrey was terrified to go home and show his father that he had even failed in the military, so he chose to fly to Miami Beach, Florida. He worked at a delicatessen and lived, for a short while, at a motel. His alcoholism would continue, and he would sink all his money into his addiction. After he was kicked out of the motel, he lived on the beach until he phoned his father and begged him to come home. Lionel would agree and Jeffrey returned to Ohio in September of 1981.

Upon returning to Ohio, his father would give him a strict set of chores and required him to find a job. He would also try to get him to stop drinking, though he was woefully unsuccessful. Within just two weeks, Jeffrey was arrested for drunk and disorderly conduct. He would serve no jail time, but this ended his time in Ohio. At this point, his father could no longer handle him, so he sent Jeffrey to West Allis, Wisconsin to live with his grandmother in December of 1981.

At first, Jeffrey would seem to have a real change, while living with his grandmother. He followed most of the house rules and even accompanied her to church. However, he could not shake his alcoholism and continued to drink. He got his first job while living there in 1982 when he became a phlebotomist at the Milwaukee Blood Plasma Center. I met someone who was taught how to draw blood by Dahmer while working at the Plasma Center. She said he was a perfectly nice person and they got along well. He would eventually be fired from his job there after he was arrested again.

On August 8, 1982, he would expose himself to twenty-five women and children at Wisconsin State Fair Park. He was arrested for indecent exposure, but again, would receive no jail time. I believe that this is one of the moments that really started to drive his descent into madness. His escalating actions suggest that he would kill again.

Jeffrey started working at the Ambrosia Chocolate Factory, as mixer, in January 1985. He would work the third shift, six days a week, with Saturday as his only day off. There is a story of Jeffrey being propositioned at the public library by another male. The man would pass Dahmer a note asking to perform fellatio on Dahmer. Jeff ignored the note, but it is believed that this would kick off his interest in finding male partners in the bath houses and gay bars of Milwaukee. How true this story is, is to be debated. I do not believe that Jeffrey ever stopped having homoerotic desires and needed to find any way to engage with them. However, he would make a distinct change and find a home in the gay red-light district of Milwaukee. This is also when he would hide in a department store to steal a mannequin, so he could fulfill his fantasies of sleeping with an unconscious man. He would sleep with the mannequin and use it as a masturbatory tool until his grandmother found it and threw it away. I have always wondered if this was truly an attempt to curb his desire to kill or if it would have only been a short-lived distraction. This begs the question: if Dahmer had had the kinds of sex dolls that we currently have, would he have continued to kill? If these dolls and competent psychological treatment are present, could we curb the desires of some of these psycho-sexual killers through a type of replacement therapy?

Towards the end of 1985, Jeffrey began frequenting bathhouses, having several sexual encounters with men. In the beginning, these encounters were mutual and typically ended in mutual one-night stands. However, this would never fulfill the fantasy that Jeffrey had. He was not interested in a willing partner, he wanted someone that he could have complete control over, and these encounters were not enough.

In June of 1986, he began drugging his partners, so he could have the experience that he was looking for. Unbeknownst to them, Jeffrey would drug their beer with a sedative and wait for them to fall asleep before having any sexual contact with their unconscious body. After being reported to the managers of the bathhouse on at least twelve occasions, they finally revoked his membership. This is when he would turn towards using hotel rooms, specifically at the Ambassador Hotel, which was only blocks away from his eventual apartment in Milwaukee. During this time, he was only drugging his victims and was not killing them, although this would not last for long. Just after he was banned, Jeffrey tried to dig up the body of an eighteen-year-old, that was recently buried, but the ground was too hard, and he gave up trying to dig. He had nothing to do with the death of this young man, but he was trying to satisfy his need to lay with an unconscious man.

Jeffrey was arrested again on September 8th, 1986, and charged with lewd and lascivious behavior for masturbating in the presence of two twelve-year-old boys. After he finally admitted to the charge, they changed it to disorderly conduct, and he was sentenced to counseling and one year of probation on March 10th, 1987.

Ten months after his sentencing, Dahmer would kill again. He met Steven Tuomi at a bar on November 20th, 1987, and invited him to a hotel room at the Ambassador Hotel. While in the hotel room, Dahmer drugged his drink and when Tuomi passed out he violated his body. Dahmer would recount that he fell asleep next to Tuomi, and when he awoke Tuomi was bruised, his chest caved in, and left dead. Dahmer had bruises all over his arms and fists but had no memory of killing him. Of course, this is not surprising since Dahmer had been blackout drunk for years. He would go out and purchase a large suitcase to transport the body to his grandmother's house. The story is, that he got a taxi to take him back to his grandmother's house and while helping him put the suitcase into the trunk the taxi driver would say something to the effect of "What do you have a body in here?" Dahmer would reply affirmatively, and they would both laugh it off, with the taxi driver not knowing that Dahmer was telling him the truth. A week later, after keeping the body in the basement of his grandmother's house, he would dismember the body, filleting the flesh off the bones. He would place the flesh in garbage bags and, just like the first murder, crush the bones with a sledgehammer. He disposed of the body in dumpsters around the city but kept the head. Dahmer would keep the head for two weeks until it was too far into the decomposition process before he then boiled it in Soilex, an industrial detergent, to take the flesh off the skull. He then bleached it and used it as a masturbatory tool until it became too brittle before he would crush it and dispose of it as well. This would be the final descent into his dark desires. From this incident, he would never return and would begin to compulsively try to fulfill his fantasies.

His next two murders happened in quick succession with almost identical results. While he lived with his grandmother, Dahmer felt a need to conceal his crimes. He would always feel a responsibility to protect his family from the depravity of his crimes. Two months after the Tuomi murder, he met and killed James Doxator, a fourteen-year-old Native American boy. He kept his body in the basement for almost a week before getting rid of the body. During that time, he would rape the dead body several times a day, until the decomposition would become so bad that it even sickened Dahmer. Just two months after that he met and killed Richard Guerrero, a twenty-two-year-old man. He would drug, strangle, and dispose of the body in a similar manner.

One month later, on April 23rd, 1988, Dahmer met Ronald Flowers. He would lure him to his grandmother's house and drug his coffee. However, his grandmother realized that Dahmer was home with another man, and Dahmer would decide to not kill Flowers. He waited until he was unconscious to take him to the hospital.

Eventually, his grandmother finally had enough and asked Jeffrey to move out in September 1988. She became tired of his drinking, bringing strange men to the house, and the putrid smells emanating from the basement and garage, where Dahmer resided. He moved to an apartment close by and was arrested two days later. He had fondled a thirteen-year-old boy, Somsack Sinthasomphone, after luring him to his apartment with a promise to pay him $50 for nude photographs. Sadly, he would not be the only person in the family that was victimized by Dahmer. As part of his trial,

Dahmer would undergo several psychological evaluations. The results showed that he had a severe feeling of alienation and impulsiveness. He was also previously diagnosed as suffering from schizoid personality disorder, a lack of interest in social relationships, detachment, and apathy. This would hinder him from developing intimate attachments to others while allowing him to live in an elaborate fantasy world. On January 30th, 1989, he plead guilty to second-degree sexual assault and enticing a child for immoral purposes. After he was convicted, he moved back in with his grandmother.

Between his conviction and sentencing, Dahmer would kill his fifth victim. He met an aspiring model, Anthony Sears, at a gay bar on March 25th, 1989. He would lure Sears to his grandmother's home, drug him, and strangle him to death. He performed the same methods to dispose of the body but would keep both the head and the genitalia. Later, Dahmer would describe Sears as "exceptionally attractive" and that was the reason he wanted to preserve him. He preserved the genitalia in acetone and placed it inside a wooden box with the head. I met Anthony Sears' cousin at a convention and had a great conversation with her about her family and this tragic moment in history. She would tell me that she wrote a paper on the most influential people in history and discussed the impact that Jeffrey Dahmer had on her family and the entire world. She thought that it was vitally important to remember the historical account of these people, so we don't repeat the same cycle. Lionel would come over to confront Jeffrey about his behavior and find the wooden box. He demanded that Jeffrey open the box and show him the contents. Jeffrey convinced him that he would open the box and show him what was inside in the morning. Of course, that night he took out the severed head and genitalia and replaced them with homosexual pornographic material. Lionel believed him and asked him to get rid of it.

He was sentenced on May 23rd, 1989, to five years' probation and one year in the House of Correction. He also had a work release so he could keep working at his job, but he had to register as a sex offender. Dahmer would serve ten months before he was released on parole. He still had to complete the five years' probation and moved back in with his grandmother, for a short time.

Dahmer would finally move into the Oxford Apartments, apartment number 213, on May 14th, 1990. This would begin a horrific series of murders that would grip the entire country for the rest of history. Within a week of moving in, he killed his sixth victim. Dahmer picked up a thirty-two-year-old prostitute named Raymond Smith, offering him $50 for sex. He would then follow his typical M.O., lacing his drink with sleeping pills and strangling him. He took polaroids of Smith's body before dismembering him and dissolved the body parts in acid and only kept the skull, spray painting it and preserving it.

A week later, Dahmer lured another victim to his apartment. This time he would lace the drink and mistakenly drink it himself. He passed out and woke up the next day missing $300, several pieces of clothing, and a watch. A few weeks after this incident, in June 1990, he would lure, drug, and strangle twenty-seven-year-old Edward Smith. This murder continued to deepen Dahmer's obsession with experimenting with the preservation process. He tried to freeze the body to remove the moisture, but it didn't work, and he then put the body in acid. He would also try to bake the skull to dry it out, but instead, it exploded in the oven.

His next victim came less than three months later, when he met a twenty-two-year-old man named Ernest Miller. Ernest would agree to go back to Dahmer's apartment for $50. This was the first account of Dahmer listening to his victim's heart and his stomach. He laced his drink with sleeping pills, but he was running out and could only put two in. Miller did not pass out completely, so Dahmer cut his throat with a knife to kill him. Dahmer later reported that he kissed and talked to the severed head, while he dismembered the rest of the body. This is more evidence that he was completely lost in his own depraved fantasy world. This would also be the first time that Dahmer would save the heart, liver, biceps, and other pieces of the body for consumption. He bleached and saved the skeleton and stripped the severed head of flesh before he painted and enameled it for preservation.

Three weeks later, on September 24th, 1990, Dahmer met David Thomas, a twenty-two-year-old man. He drugged him, before strangling him to death and dismembering the body but would not keep any of his parts. He only took pictures of his body and saved them. After this murder, Dahmer would not kill anyone for almost five months. However, this doesn't mean that Dahmer was not on the hunt. He would unsuccessfully try to lure at least five men to his apartment.

It is interesting to note that during this time Dahmer was also attending his counseling appointments and reporting severe bouts of anxiety and depression. No doubt, this was attributed to his fear of being caught and dealing with the emotions that he thought he should be having because of his murders. He also mentioned that he often had suicidal thoughts. This is something that we often do not talk about in the cycle of a serial killer. We all know that they struggle with compulsive feelings to fulfill their fantasy. This is the reason that they continue to kill over and over. However, after the murder happens, the reality of the situation never lives up to the fantasy that they have in their head. This leads to inevitable depression and often suicidal thoughts. It may even lead to suicide attempts, but the narcissistic part of them often cannot follow through, and they are thrust right back into the cycle on repeat until they are stopped.

In 1991, Dahmer murdered an additional six men before being caught. His first victim was seventeen-year-old Curtis

Straughter. He would lure him with money to pose for nude photographs, strangle him with a leather strap, dismember him, and take photos of each stage of the dismembering process. Two months later, on April 7th, he lured the nineteen-year-old Errol Lindsey to his apartment. This was the first time that Dahmer would experiment with creating a willing sex zombie. He drugged Errol, drilled a hole in his skull, and injected his brain with hydrochloric acid. Errol would wake up once complaining of a headache before Dahmer would drug him again, and then dismember his body. He would try and retain his skin, but he was unable to and had to dispose of it.

It was about this time that other residents of the Oxford Apartments began to complain to the management about the smells coming from apartment 213. Dahmer would initially tell him that his refrigerator went out and the meat in it went bad. The landlord came to the apartment and helped Dahmer clean the fridge. He did not notice anything odd and hoped that the problem was taken care of. When there were further complaints, Dahmer would say that his fish had died, and he had neglected to clean the fish tank.

On May 24th, 1991, Dahmer met Tony Hughes at a nightclub. This is the victim that was the focus of episode six of the Netflix show. The show took many creative liberties, showing an ongoing relationship between Tony and Jeffrey. They would even go as far as to show Jeffrey trying to have a "normal" relationship with Tony. However, this is far from the reality of the encounter between Dahmer and Hughes. In most of the accounts from family and friends, Tony Hughes frequented some of the same clubs that Dahmer did and may have run into him, but it was far from an ongoing relationship. The truth is they probably only met in passing and the night of Tony's unfortunate death was the first time that they had ever spent any time together. Dahmer would lure him back to the apartment with the offer to pose for photographs. He would then drug Hughes and attempt to drill into his skull to turn him into a willing partner, but Tony died in the process.

Just two days later, Dahmer picked up fourteen-year-old Konerak Sinthasomphone, the younger brother of the child he molested just three years before. Dahmer would lure him in the same way. He drugged him and led him into the bedroom, where the bloating body of Tony Hughes was still lying on the floor. When Konerak passed out, Dahmer performed oral sex on him. He then drilled a hole in the front of his skull, injecting straight into the frontal lobe. Later that night, Dahmer would leave the apartment to go and get more beer. When he returned, in the early morning hours, Konerak was sitting outside naked trying to speak with three women. Dahmer tried to tell them that he was a drunk friend and led him back into the apartment. The women had already called 9-1-1. When the police arrived, Dahmer would tell them that he was his drunk nineteen-year-old boyfriend. This was at the height of the AIDS epidemic, which was believed to be the gay plague at the time. The women tried to point out the injuries that Konerak had sustained but to no avail. The police would even tell them to mind their own business. Although Konerak seemed to try and struggle away from Dahmer, they still allowed Dahmer to take him back into the apartment. During that time, the fire department arrived. One of the firemen recommended that Konerak go in for treatment. He was bleeding from the head, had blood on his testicles, and was bleeding from his rectum. The response from the police was to tell the fire department to leave and would even escort Konerak and Dahmer back to the apartment. Dahmer showed them the polaroids he took of Konerak, but one of the officers smelled something strange. It was the decomposing body of Tony Hughes, but the officer just peeked into the bedroom and didn't really investigate. So they left and listed the incident as a domestic dispute. After the police left, Dahmer would administer a second injection into Konerak's brain, killing him. Dahmer took the next day off from work to dismember the bodies of both Konerak and Hughes.

From June 30th to July 19th, 1991, Dahmer would kill four victims. It started with twenty-year-old Matt Turner, whom he met at a bus station in Chicago and lured to the apartment under the guise of a professional photo shoot. On July 5th, he would get twenty-three-year-old Jeremiah Weinberger to come home with him for a weekend of fun. He would end up pouring boiling water into his brain, sending him into a coma, and he would die two days later. Ten days later he met twenty-four-year-old Oliver Lacy and lured him with posing nude for photographs. He would try and prolong his time with Oliver by using chloroform, but it didn't work, so he ended up strangling him. He dismembered him and placed both his head and heart in the refrigerator. Four days later, he was fired from his job at the chocolate factory and immediately went out to find twenty-five-year-old Joseph Bradehoft. He left Joseph lying on his bed for two days before trying to clean up, and by that time, he would be covered in maggots. He would clean up, dismember the body, and place the head in the refrigerator.

Two days later, on July 21st, 1991, Dahmer offered three men $100 to pose for nude photographs. Traci Edwards, a thirty-two-year-old man, took him up on his offer. When they arrived at Dahmer's apartment, Edwards immediately smelled a terrible odor. Edwards turned to look at the tropical fish tank and Dahmer placed a handcuff on one of his wrists, but Edwards began to struggle; Dahmer was unable to get the cuff on his other wrist. Dahmer assured him that it was just part of the photography and led him into the bedroom. Edwards would later recount that he saw nude pictures on his walls and realized that the smell was coming from a fifty-five-gallon drum in the corner. Dahmer turned on *The Exorcist III*, which was one of the rituals he would use before drugging and killing his victims. Dahmer then pulled a knife on Edwards and threatened him. In an incredible move of bravery, Edwards would agree to take off his clothes and pose for the pictures, but only if he would put away the knife and take off the handcuffs. Dahmer ignored him and began watching the movie. Edwards told the police that he watched Dahmer enter a trance-like state, where he was rocking back and forth, chanting with the movie. He then turned his attention back to Edwards, placing his head on his chest trying to listen to his heart. Dahmer would then tell Edwards that he was going to eat his heart. Edwards eventually talked Dahmer into going back into the living room, where he felt he had a better chance to escape. He asked to use the bathroom, and when Dahmer released control of the handcuffs, Edwards punched him in the face and ran out the front door.

When Edwards got out of the apartment building, he flagged down two Milwaukee police officers. He tried to get them to take off his handcuffs, but the cuffs were a different brand, and their keys did not fit. Edwards would have to accompany the police back to Dahmer's apartment to get the key to unlock the cuffs. Dahmer invited all three of them into the apartment and told the police that the key was in his bedside table. The officer walked into the bedroom and saw the knife under the bed, that Edwards had claimed Dahmer had pulled on him. Dahmer would try and retrieve the key before the officer had an opportunity to open the drawer, but the officer would stop him, telling him to back off. They then discovered the polaroids that showed his victims in various stages of dismemberment and decomposition. At that point, the police tried to place Dahmer under arrest, and he would resist but in short order, they had him on the ground with his hands cuffed behind his back. One of the officers would then open the refrigerator to find the severed head of one of his recent victims. By the time the search of the apartment had concluded, they would find four severed heads in the kitchen, seven skulls in the bedroom and closet, two human hearts and pieces of an arm muscle in the refrigerator, an entire torso and bag of human organs in the freezer, two complete skeletons, a pair of severed hands, two preserved penises, a scalp that was mummified, three torsos dissolving in the fifty-five-gallon drum, and seventy-four polaroid pictures of his victims.

During the following two weeks, Dahmer confessed to seventeen murders in total, sixteen in Wisconsin and one in Ohio. He would confess to necrophilia, cannibalism, drugging, strangling, and dismembering his victims. Dahmer described his methods and reasoning for all his crimes. He would tell them that he ingested his victims because he wanted them to always be a part of him, and that his obsession with picking up and killing these men was so insistent that it was all he could think about. He would explain that he kept the bones because he wanted to erect an altar where he could meditate and draw power from their deaths.

Dahmer was charged with fifteen murders, excluding the murder of Steven Tuomi for which they had no evidence, and who Dahmer had no memory of murdering. He was also not charged with the attempted murder of Traci Edwards. Dahmer would plead guilty but insane to fifteen of the murders he was charged with. The trial would become beset by three psychiatrists. The one for the defense believed that Dahmer suffered from severe mental disorders including necrophilia, borderline personality disorder, schizotypal personality disorder, alcoholism, and a generalized psychotic disorder. The prosecution brought on two psychiatrists, and both would testify that Dahmer had no mental defect or disease. They both testified that Dahmer knew right from wrong, that he planned out his crimes, and that he used his alcoholism to deal with the emotions of committing his heinous crimes. On February 15th, 1992, the jury delivered their verdict. They determined that Dahmer was sane for all fifteen murders and not suffering from any mental disease. Two days later at his sentencing, Dahmer addressed the court, mentioning that he wished for death, claiming that none of the murders were motivated by hate, and finally stated that he knew that none of the families could ever forgive him for what he had done. He was given fifteen life sentences plus 930 years. The state of Wisconsin had abolished the death penalty, so it was never an option for Dahmer. He would be given his sixteenth life sentence on May 1st, 1992, in Ohio for the murder of Steven Hicks.

While in prison Dahmer would become a Christian and was baptized in May 1994. He would also do several famous interviews during this time. The infamy of his crimes made him a celebrity in the prison and he began to receive tons of mail. It seemed that Dahmer would start to relish this infamy and the other prisoners started to take exception to it. On July 3rd, 1994, the first attempt was made on Dahmer's life, when Osvaldo Durruthy would attempt to slice Dahmer's throat with a razor blade embedded in a toothbrush, after the weekly church service.

On November 28th, 1994, Dahmer began his work detail cleaning the prison gym. He was left alone for twenty minutes with two other inmates, Jesse Anderson and Christopher Scarver. When the prison guards returned, they found both Dahmer and Anderson beaten and dying after Christopher Scarver bludgeoned them with a barbell. Dahmer died an hour later at a nearby hospital. Anderson lasted two days but eventually succumbed to the head trauma and passed away as well. Scarver would claim that God told him to kill both men. He would kill Dahmer first, who evidently did not even struggle, as if he had accepted his fate. However, Anderson struggled and had many defense wounds from trying to preserve his own life. There is some speculation on why Dahmer didn't struggle. Did Scarver catch him by surprise? Did Dahmer accept his fate as just punishment for his crimes? Or did he believe that he was right with God and ready to face his maker? We will never know the reasons why Dahmer reacted the way that he did in his final moments, but I believe it may have been a combination of the last two. It seems in the final years of Dahmer's life, he had legitimately converted to Christianity, and not your normal jailhouse conversion, but a real belief and acknowledgment of his own psychosis. In his own conversion, he may have felt a need to be punished for all the damage that he created throughout his life. Thus, willfully accepting the punishment that Christopher Scarver would dish out on that fateful day.

Myth #1: Dahmer Was Always a Class Clown

While in high school Jeffrey Dahmer was considered many different things by different people. He would be a figure, much like any of us, who was struggling to find a way to fit in. Often people who commit the crimes that he later committed have lifelong anti-social personalities. However, we find that Jeffrey had friends in high school, but he also had people who were repulsed by him and counted him as an outcast.

By the time Dahmer was fourteen years old and beginning high school, he was a full-blown alcoholic. He was drinking, at all hours of the day. He brought bottles of liquor to school and would drink before, during, and after classes. In the first two years of high school, he was maintaining well and even kept his grades at an acceptable level. He was already a functioning alcoholic. Some of his fellow students considered him an outcast because of his drunkenness, but there was another group of kids who loved the fact that Dahmer could get them alcohol.

Contrary to some articles you might read, Dahmer was never a classically "popular" teenager. He was not seen as a type of class clown, but more of a pariah by most of the other students. He was someone that the kids snickered at, like watching a car accident, rather than thinking he was the life of the party. In high school Jeffrey would do impressions that were often very offensive, dealing with handicapped people or other people with mental disabilities. He would play pranks on other children and his closest friends would form the Dahmer Fan Club. It was not really a group of friends, but rather a bunch of kids that followed Dahmer around waiting for him to do the next outlandish thing. Dahmer was the kid who showed no fear, who would take any bet, and who would fall down faking a seizure for attention. He would do this so often that the other students would call it "Doing a Dahmer." For most of the kids that went to school with him, this was not a term of endearment, but for the Dahmer Fan Club, it would be just another good laugh.

What we should remember, regarding the Dahmer Fan Club or his "friends," is that they would follow him around and allow him to do all the things they wouldn't or were too scared to do, but they were not a support system for him. Often when we have friends, they become a support system of people that we can rely on, share our struggles, and help us get back on track when we stray. The Dahmer Fan Club were none of these things. The truth is, they really didn't know Dahmer at all. He was just the crazy kid that would do anything and give them a good laugh. Dahmer would never share the collection of dead animals, his process for taking the flesh off the bones, or his obsession with unconscious men. The reason we know this for sure is because it was only three weeks after his graduation from high school when Dahmer killed his first victim. It would be fourteen years and seventeen victims later before any of Dahmer's "friends" would know anything about the true desires that he was struggling with. It would completely change their perspective on their teenage years. In interviews, many of them express a feeling of being hit by a brick wall when the crimes of Jeffrey Dahmer were revealed. They would question all the things that they thought they believed. If they could spend time with someone so depraved and have no clue, what else in their lives did they miss? It is certainly a sobering reminder to pay attention to the things going on around us.

Myth #2: Dahmer Only Killed Ethnic Men

There has always been the prevailing belief that Dahmer only killed African American or ethnic homosexual men. There have been many memes and comedy skits based on this thought process. Consequently, there are people that have assumed that Dahmer was racist and wanted to eradicate ethnic people. Somehow, we miss what Dahmer himself said about this. In his interview with Stone Phillips, in 1994, Dahmer admits that his only motivation was to find the most attractive person to him, he didn't care about their sexual orientation or their race. If anything, this shows the systemic racism that was prevalent in our culture during that time given the fact that the police refused to investigate the crimes against both ethnic people and gay people several times, which is deplorable.

In fact, Dahmer killed across the board, with White, Asian, Native American, Mexican, and African American victims. However, upon looking at all seventeen victims, he would seem to be attracted to ethnic people more than anyone else. Dahmer did not kill because of hate, he killed because of abandonment. He wanted these men to remain with him forever, and as soon as they wanted to leave, he was unable to allow them to do that. He would kill them and then try to preserve their bodies to keep them longer. He would eventually resort to cannibalism because he believed that it would make them a part of him. So, from a very macabre point of view, Dahmer loved people of other ethnicities. He desired them so much he would kill them, in an attempt to keep the beauty of that ethnicity with him forever.

There is also some debate on whether Dahmer chose his victims because he knew that those groups would be overlooked by the police and never be investigated. There are certainly some killers who are extremely intelligent and plan out their kills, attempting to avert capture. I don't feel like this fits the profile of Jeffrey Dahmer. He seems honest in his admittance to choosing these men because he was attracted to them. Dahmer was a lust killer, who had little regard for anything but his own sexual desires, which ultimately led him to kill. The rampage of Jeffrey Dahmer became a serious failure of the police, who were notified several times of his strange behavior and the smells from his apartment, and even gave victims back to him. Their unwillingness to protect the gay community of Milwaukee is awful. We must also remember that these crimes happened during the AIDS epidemic of the 1980s. During that time, it was believed to be the "gay plague." Although this is not an excuse for the police to ignore the crimes in the homosexual community, it certainly played a part in the fear of investigating these crimes. When we look at many of these cases, it becomes a sad commentary on the state of the law enforcement community. We certainly need our law enforcement, but we need them to be trained appropriately, given the right resources, and to be held accountable for their actions. One of the things I have always wondered, is if Dahmer would have had a truly fulfilling relationship with another consenting adult, would he have continued killing? In a short answer, I believe that eventually, it would have always led to this end. I do not believe that anyone would have been able to escape his psychosis. He would have eventually found a reason to commit the crime, only because I do not believe that he would have ever been able to accept the help that he truly needed. With that being said, if Dahmer brought his victims home because he wanted to find someone whom he could love who would love him back, would it be possible to change his destructive pattern, if that void in his life was filled? This is where intensive, directed, and honest therapy could have played a major part in curbing Dahmer's behavior. If he had been able to find a community that accepted him as a homosexual male, who was into domination and submission and had been allowed to explore those desires in a safe and consenting environment, maybe we would have been able to help him find a different outlet for his dark desires. One of the reasons desires become an obsession, is because we get a thrill from hiding them and feeling like they are taboo. Once the mysticism is gone, those desires often lose their power over us. I know many people, in the oddities community, that love to play with bones and enjoy taxidermy, who have incredibly fulfilling relationships. But I believe that we must draw the line when those interests begin to hurt other people.

Again, in the time and culture that Dahmer lived in, he would never have been able to get the necessary help for his trauma. By the time he started killing again, he was unable to stop, and the obsession had completely taken over. However, this is just food for thought and a stark reminder of why it is important to have knowledge of these people and their crimes. We can learn a great deal and equip ourselves with the tools to identify these people, create programs to help people who are struggling with their dark desires, and save other families from facing the tragedy that these killers bring.

Myth #3: Dahmer Needed to Be Drunk to Kill His Victims

I have already mentioned the many psychotherapists and their varying theories at the trial of Jeffrey Dahmer. There were some who believed that he had many mental disorders, while others believed he had none. They also dealt with his alcoholism differently. They would debate over whether he drank because of his crimes or in spite of them. What we know for sure is that Jeffrey was drinking early in his life. Although, we don't know exactly when he began drinking or why, we do know that by high school he was a fully functioning alcoholic. It is believed that he began drinking to deal with his feelings of homosexuality. In the mid-70s, when Dahmer was discovering his feelings about other men it was unacceptable in our society. It was seen as a disease. You would be shunned by the church, you could be disowned by your family, and physically assaulted by people in school and outside. I believe that this could have been a contributing factor to why Jeffrey began drinking, but certainly not the sole reason. He would be the next in a long line of alcoholics on his mother's side of the family. We now know that alcoholism is a disease and that Jeffrey would just attempt to drown the feelings that he was unable to express in his drunkenness.

The very fact that his drinking started long before his killing began seems to indicate that he drank in spite of killing rather than because of it. If Dahmer did drink to deal with the many traumatic things that he faced in his life, it could be seen that he used it as a coping mechanism. Does that mean that he also used it to place himself in an alternate state of mind, so he could engage in his killing behavior? That would be the exact question that the court would grapple with.

Most of us enjoy a good social drink. We use it to loosen up, wind down from a difficult day at the office, or as social lubrication so we are more willing to open up and talk to other people. This, however, is not how Dahmer drank. He used drinking to help other people get into that state of mind, as well as to drug them, but by the time Dahmer came back from the military, he had been an alcoholic for over ten years. It had become an integral part of his life, and he would be unable to function without it. While he was in Florida, he lost his room at the hotel because he was more interested in drinking than needing a roof over his head. This was someone so deep in his addiction that there was no life without it. Sadly, this would not be the only addiction that Dahmer couldn't live without. If anyone has dealt with an alcoholic family member, you know the struggle. The scary part is that Dahmer would also be able to function "normally." He was able to hold a job, and in fact, it seems that the reason why he lost his jobs was not because of drinking but mainly because he would be arrested for sex charges.

Dahmer didn't need to drink to commit his crimes Dahmer had to drink to function at all. His body was so dependent on alcohol to function, that if he didn't have a drink he would go through severe withdrawal. However, his drinking may have allowed him to stay numb enough to continue living in the depraved nightmare that he had created. Most of us would not be able to stomach dismembering seventeen people. Dahmer did it, as if in a trance. This suggests, not a drunken haze, but a serious mental disorder that would allow him to suspend any empathy or identification with humanity he might have. With these significant mental disorders, and without any real intensive therapy, Dahmer would have found a way to kill no matter what. He needed the alcohol to survive and needed to fulfill the obsessive fantasies that he had.

Legend: Dahmer Killed an 18th Victim

Since the arrest of Jeffrey Dahmer in 1991, people have always wondered if there were more victims. Could it be that Dahmer had only strangled, dismembered, and disposed of only seventeen men? What happened in the nine years between the first murder of Steven Hicks and his second murder of Steven Tuomi? We know that Dahmer dropped out of college and was discharged by the military, but was it really for a lack of time or desire?

What really happened in the seven months he spent in Miami, Florida in 1981? We know that he worked at a delicatessen and lived at a motel until he could no longer pay for it. He then lived on the beach until he decided to go back home to Ohio, but is that really all that happened there? We also know that the only other time that Dahmer lived on his own would be right after his graduation, and he killed Steven Hicks at that time. So could Jeffrey Dahmer, who was fresh out of the military, really go seven months unsupervised without killing someone?

At the Hollywood Mall in Hollywood, Florida, on July 27th, 1991, six-year-old Adam Walsh was shopping at Sears with his mother. His mother would go to inquire about a lamp that was for sale, leaving Adam with some other boys to play an Atari 2600 that was on display. While she was gone, the boys would end up being escorted out of the store because they had gotten into a fight, while taking turns to play. It is believed that Adam was abducted outside the entrance to the mall, where the security guard led the boys.

His mother would spend the next ninety minutes looking for him in the store before finally calling the police at 1:55 p.m. Adam Walsh would never be seen alive again and his severed head was found two weeks later in a drainage ditch. This was the son of, now famous, John Walsh, who would create the show *America's Most Wanted*. He created it in response to his outrage over the number of unsolved criminal cases throughout America. He is a man who decided to use his tragedy and turn it into a positive way to help prevent other families from facing the same thing he faced.

The case is currently closed, and they have identified a suspect. It still has never gone to trial, and no one has ever been convicted of the kidnapping and murder of Adam Walsh. Ottis Toole would initially confess to the crime and later retract his confession. He was very detailed in his description of the crime. He said that he abducted him because he wanted to make Adam his adopted son. He lured him into the car with candy and toys, and he began to drive north towards Jacksonville. Adam would begin to panic, and Toole would knock him out with several punches to the face. He would take him to a deserted service road, drag him out of the car, and cut his head off with a machete. He would then take his body and burn it in an old refrigerator in Jacksonville. Ottis Tootle and Henry Lee Lucas admitted to hundreds of crimes and led investigators on wild goose chases all over the country. Many of those confessions were easily disproved, and some of the people believed to be murdered were even still alive. Currently, Ottis is considered by the police to be the killer of Adam Walsh though it is still contested by many in the true crime field. In the case of Adam Walsh, the police did a terrible job of handling the evidence. They lost the blood-stained carpet from the car that Toole was thought to have driven, the machete that Toole admitted to using to cut off Adam's head, and they would even lose the car itself. The only reason that Toole was not tried for the killing was because he died in prison on September 15th, 1996.

After Jeffrey Dahmer was arrested in 1991, he became a suspect in the Adam Walsh kidnapping and murder. Lionel Dahmer called the *America's Most Wanted* hotline after their episode on Adam Walsh. He knew that Dahmer had been living in the area and by this time, he knew his son was a pedophile. In fact, Miami Beach is only forty-five minutes away from the mall that Adam Walsh was kidnapped from. There were two eyewitnesses who placed Dahmer at the mall the day that Adam was abducted. One of those witnesses would claim that he saw Dahmer throw a child into a blue van, and there were reports that Dahmer had access to a blue van at the job that he was working at. Before Dahmer's death in 1994, he was asked about the murder of Adam Walsh. Dahmer would deny having anything to do with the abduction or murder. He said that he had already admitted to so many other crimes, why would he not admit to this further crime? John Walsh, himself would say that he found no evidence that Dahmer had anything to do with the kidnapping and murder of his son. However, many other people felt that Dahmer was hesitant to comment on the Walsh murder because it would label him a pedophile in prison and that would be a death sentence. Although Dahmer did kill a boy as young as fourteen years old, which would classify him as a pedophile, he always said that he believed he was older. The admission of killing a boy who was only six years old would be undeniable proof of this. Little did he know his admittance wouldn't matter; he already had a death sentence, which Christopher Scarver would carry out.

We will never know for certain who kidnapped and murdered Adam Walsh. Was it Ottis Toole or Jeffrey Dahmer who committed this horrific crime? There was evidence that could prove the murder, but it was lost. The evidence on Jeffrey Dahmer is circumstantial, at best. At this point, both suspects are dead and buried, and unless a suspect who is currently unnamed steps forward, we will never know the truth. The crime will go down in history as credited to Ottis Toole. It is also possible that Dahmer could have been involved in other murders, of which we know nothing about.

Podcasts
- *Murder Metal Mayhem* - Bonus Ep – "Apartment 213"
- *TimeSuck w/ Dan Cummins* - Ep. 36 – "Jeffrey Dahmer: The Cannibal of Milwaukee"
- *Last Podcast on the Left* - Eps. 122-124
- *Mind of a Monster: Jeffrey Dahmer* Podcast

Books
- *Dahmer's Confession* by John Borowski
- *A Father's Story* by Lionel Dahmer
- *Dahmer The Psych Reports* by Taylor James
- *Jeffrey Dahmer: A Terrifying True Story of Rape, Murder, and Cannibalism* by Jack Rosewood
- *My Friend Dahmer* by Derf Backderf
- *Monster: The True Story of the Jeffrey Dahmer Murders* by Anne E. Schwartz

Documentaries & Movies
- *Conversations with a Killer: The Jeffrey Dahmer Tapes* (2022)
- *Mind of a Monster* (2020)
- *Dahmer* (2022) - Netflix
- Jeffrey Dahmer Interviews - YouTube

CHAPTER TEN

Dennis Rader is an interesting addition to the list of serial killers throughout the ages and the only one that I have spoken to personally. For this chapter of the book, I was able to ask Dennis what he would like me to cover, and he gave me the legend that he has been interrogated about several times. It is a recent case, as he was caught less than twenty years ago, in 2005. He, like the Zodiac before him, wrote letters to the police and taunted them. He led a double life, where he lived out his dark desires in one life and lived another where he was a family man, with a wife and children. Serial killers who can pull off the "normal" life, along with their deep fantasy life, are in the minority. Dennis gave himself the nickname B.T.K. (Bind, Torture, Kill), becoming a sexual sadist and cross-dresser, who killed at least ten people. Although he killed anyone that got in his way, including men and children, he would initially target women. He would also differentiate himself by taking a thirteen-year hiatus from killing, and then return to pick up like he never left.

Dennis Rader was born on March 9th, 1945. Most of the biographies will tell you that Dennis was born in Pittsburg, Kansas; however, upon talking with Dennis, he says that he was actually born in Columbus, Kansas, about thirty minutes away. His parents were largely absent during his childhood, leaving Dennis and his three brothers to their own devices. Dennis described feeling abandoned by his mother and he resented her for the way that she treated him. By this time, the family was living in Wichita. Dennis struggled, from an early age, with disturbing sexual fantasies. He would cut out women from magazine ads and add bondage materials to the pictures, and carry them around with him, using them for masturbation. It was later reported that when he was spanked as a child, he would get extremely aroused. He would get excited reading about murders, and much like Bundy, the True Detective Magazines would turn him on. He would masturbate with a book that his father had on the Lonely Hearts Killers. He would describe to Katherine Ramsland that he would often play cowboys and Indians with his friends in local silos. During these times of play, they would tie each other up and Dennis would become sexually aroused by the ropes. This would lead him to a childhood fantasy about tying a woman to the train tracks and watching her get run over by a train. Later in his life, he would draw up a map of a torture silo that he wanted to create, where he could take his victims to do as he pleased.

Often his childhood is regarded as typical for the time, with traditional values. However, his own behaviors suggest something very different. The fact that Dennis harbored deviant sexual behavior from a very early age suggests some serious physical and possibly sexual abuse. In an interview, Dennis' daughter, Kerri Rawson, said that her father would always deny being abused in any way during his childhood. As young children, we emulate the things that we see since we have little frame of reference for the world around us. It is not possible for our impressionable minds to come up with elaborate sexual fantasies organically on our own. There must have been something or someone that gave him experience with such things. It could be something small that his mind chose to sexualize, and as obsession sets in it became part of his being. Dennis shared a story with Katherine Ramsland that during his childhood, his mother got her wedding ring stuck on a spring in the couch and she could not get her hand out. She would ask Dennis to get help, seeming terrified to Dennis. In a crazy turn of events, this became a pivotal moment in his life. From this moment on, Dennis would long to trap women and have them look at him in terror, and this excitement would drive him. Could this truly be the moment that shaped his twisted destiny?

In another similarity to Bundy, Dennis would start peeping on his neighbors early in his life. He would also steal articles of clothing, that he would wear while he was peeping. This would be a practice that he would carry on his entire life, even dressing up in his victim's clothing and applying self-bondage for his sexual release, between murders. When he would do this, his sexual fantasy would involve him becoming his victim and acting out the bondage he performed.

After a mediocre high school career, Dennis went into the United States Air Force. He served four years in the military and learned much of the discipline that would help him commit the crimes. About a year later, he married Paula

Dietz on May 22nd, 1971. By 1979, Dennis graduated from college with a Bachelor of Science degree with a major in the Administration of Justice. He used this knowledge to try to avoid some of the common investigation techniques police would use and from the years 1974 to 1988, Dennis worked for ADT Security Services as an installer. He used this job to case out some of his victims and learn the ins and outs of security systems, as well as steal articles of clothing that would fuel his sexual desires.

The first set of murders that Rader committed occurred on January 15th, 1974. On this day, he killed four members of the Otero family: Joseph Sr. (thirty-eight), Julie (thirty-three), Joey (nine), and Josie (eleven). Rader cased the family for approximately two months before he decided to act. Although his main target was Julie Otero, he killed everyone in the home as collateral damage. Even though he meticulously planned his crimes, he did not plan for the two kids and the husband to be home on the day of the murders. Rader cut the phone lines not knowing that the husband and kids were also home. Joey opened the door to let out the dog and Rader would use that moment to enter the house and hold the family at gunpoint. He took them into the bedroom and began tying them up, placing a bag over Joseph's head, who would end up slowly suffocating to death. He would then strangle Julie to death with a rope that he tightened around her throat. He would then place several bags over Joey's head and watch as he struggled and suffocated to death. Finally, he led Josie down to the basement, where he hung her from a pipe with a noose. He would also masturbate and leave semen close to her body in the basement. When the three older Otero children came home from school, they found the bodies of their family.

Rader's next victim, Kathryn Bright, was attacked on April 4th, 1974. Rader broke into the house through the back door and waited for Kathryn to arrive. Again, Rader was surprised. After all his research and watching his "projects," her brother Kevin Bright would unexpectedly come home with her that day. He would hold them both at gunpoint, telling them that he was a wanted criminal and that he just needed their car, food, and some money. Rader forced them both into the bedroom and instructed Kevin to bind his sister with the rope. Later in court, Rader would brag that if he had brought his own rope, neither of them would have survived. Rader took Kevin to the next room and attempted to tie him up. However, Kevin struggled, trying to fight Rader for the gun, nearly getting it away from him, but instead, he was shot twice in the head. Rader left him for dead and went back to work on Kathryn. Kathryn also fought, getting some of BTK's DNA under her fingernails, which would end up becoming very helpful in convicting Rader of this murder. In the process of strangling her, Rader heard Kevin running out the front door. At that moment, Rader realized that he could not take his time as he had planned, and stabbed Kathryn multiple times in the abdomen. Rader believed that the police were already on their way, so he cleaned up the best he could and ran away from the crime scene. Kathryn would face multiple surgeries but ultimately succumbed to her wounds. Kevin would be left in critical condition but would survive the encounter.

After several months, in October 1974, the police arrested three men and charged them with the Otero murders. Rader, being an extreme narcissist, could not let someone else take the credit for a murder that he committed. Rader called the Wichita Eagle newspaper and spoke to Don Granger, telling him that the "real" killer left a letter in a mechanical engineering textbook at the public library. This letter would include specific details that only the real killer would know, and it has never been released to the public in full, though there are excerpts that have been released and can be found online. This letter is also where Rader gives himself the name B.T.K., writing in the postscript, "P.S. Since sex criminals do not change their M.O. or by nature cannot do so, I will not change mine. The code words for me will be… Bind them, torture them, kill them, B.T.K., you see he at it again. They will be on the next victim."

After that letter, Rader would wait two and a half years before he would kill again. On March 17th, 1977, Rader attempted to fulfill "Project Green," but when he knocked on the door no one answered. So, he continued to search for a random victim. Upon searching the neighborhood, he met a five-year-old boy named Steve Relford. Rader showed him a picture of his family and asked the boy if he knew where they lived. Steve said he couldn't help him and then left to go home, but Rader followed the boy to find out where he lived. Rader would try another house before he went to Steve's home, but when he knocked no one answered the door. When he knocked on their door again, another boy answered, and Rader identified himself as a private detective to gain entry to the home. Once he was in the home, Rader pulled out his 357 Magnum, just as Shirley Vian came out of the bedroom. He told her that he had sexual fantasies and would need to tie her up and take pictures of her. He attempted to tie up the children, but they began to cry, so instead he locked the three of them in the bathroom, telling them that if they tried to escape, he would blow their heads off. He also left toys and blankets in the bathroom to make the children as comfortable as possible. After securing both bathroom doors, he went back to tie up Shirley Vian. As he was tying her up, Shirley vomited on herself, and Rader would help her clean up and get her a glass of water. He even took time to comfort her before he finished tying her up, put a plastic bag over her head, and strangled her to death with a rope. The police would later find her panties next to her on the bed with traces of Rader's semen on them. The kids were yelling and banging on the bathroom door when the phone rang. Rader then remembered that a neighbor was going to check on the family, so he gathered up his kill kit and left the residence.

Eight months later, Rader would see Nancy Jo Fox going into her residence, and mark her as a "project," before he began stalking her every move. He made his move on December 8th, 1977, when he knocked on the door, but no one answered. He cut the phone lines and then broke into the residence, waiting in her kitchen for her to arrive home. Rader would consider this his perfect "hit" and the "most enjoyable." When she arrived home Rader confronted her at gunpoint and told her that he had a sexual problem and would need to tie her up and rape her. They talked for a short while before Nancy said let's get this over with so I can call the police. She asked to use the bathroom and Rader would allow her to but requested that she undress before she came out. When she came out of the bathroom Rader handcuffed her and tied her feet, before taking off his belt to strangle her with it. As he was strangling her, he finally revealed who he was, just to see the terror that would come across her face as she realized. Rader would then masturbate over the body leaving his semen on her nightgown next to the body. The next day, Rader called the police and let them know that there was a murder that had been committed, and the victim was Nancy Jo Fox.

Rader sent his second communication to the media in January 1978, sending a parody poem to the Wichita Eagle about the murder of Shirley Vian. A month later another letter was sent to KAKE-TV where he claimed seven murders and discussed his intent to kill again. In the four-page letter, he detailed his sexual gratification at the death of the Otero child, including a poem entitled "Oh! Death to Nancy," and a drawing of the Nancy Fox crime scene. He even suggested several different names for himself, including the infamous B.T.K. It was in this letter he would say, "How many do I have to kill before I get a name in the paper or some national attention?" This is where we really get to see some of the extreme narcissistic traits of Rader. He wants to be known as the smartest and worst killer of all time. This would also be the first time that Rader mentioned "Factor X," which would be, what he believed, took him over, allowing him to kill. It is very similar to the idea of "the Entity" that Bundy would describe in interviews.

Rader had many "projects" that he would follow, but he would only attempt one more murder in the 1970s. He broke into the house of Anna Williams in April 1979. Rader would wait for hours in her house, but she did not come home. Anna was out with friends and decided to stay out late; this decision would save her life. He became increasingly angry when she did not come home, and in his impatience, he would leave with his plans unfulfilled.

It was six years before Rader would murder again, but on April 27th, 1985, B.T.K. would strike again. By this time, Rader had two kids, was a Boy Scout troop leader, and was involved in his local church. By all accounts, he was living the life of a normal family man, but Rader was harboring some dark, terrible secrets. He was forty years old and needed to kill again. Marine Hedge was a fifty-three-year-old widow and lived only a block away from Rader in Park City, Kansas. Rader was in the middle of a Scout meeting when he complained of a headache and needed to leave. He walked back to the bowling alley where he left his car, ordered a beer, swished it around in his mouth, and spilled a little on himself. He wanted people to think that he was a little drunk to help his alibi. He then immediately took a taxi back to Park City. He went to the Hedge residence, assuming that she was home. Rader cut the phone lines and entered through the back door. When he realized that she was not home, he decided he would wait in the bedroom until she returned home. When her car pulled up, she was not alone, she had a man with her. Rader would then hide in the bedroom closet until around 1:00 a.m. when the man left, and Marine had fallen asleep. He would then attack her and choke her to death, before He then took her body, loaded it into the trunk of her car, and drove to Christ Lutheran

Church, where he attended services. He blacked out the windows and dragged the body into the basement where he took photographs of the body in bondage and different positions. He then loaded Marine's body back up into her car and dumped her off a dirt road not far from his home. The police found her body on May 5th, 1985.

Rader's next "project" named "PJ" would be fully realized on September 16th, 1986. He had been stalking her, by walking by her house and listening to her play piano. On that day, Rader dressed up like a telephone repairman and came knocking on Vicki Wegerle's door. She would let him in thinking that he was going to repair the telephone line, instead, he would cut the line. He then held her at gunpoint and let her know that he was going to tie her up. He led her to the bedroom, where he attempted to bind her, but she fought back. In the fight for her life, she cut and scratched Rader, getting his DNA under her fingernails. Sadly, she would lose the fight when Rader choked her with a nylon stocking that was in her bedroom. He then took photos of her body in different positions and left, also stealing her car. Vicki's husband, Bill, was returning home and saw his wife's car driving away from the home. When he arrived at the house, he found his two-year-old in the living room alone. Upon searching for his wife, he found her on the floor behind their bed, still alive, and the paramedics attempted to revive her, but sadly she passed away from her injuries on the way to the hospital. Rader would dump the car a few blocks away from the house and walk home.

The final known victim of B.T.K. would die five years later on January 19th, 1991. Delores Davis was sixty-two years old and lived a mile and a half away from Rader's home. He was going on a camping weekend with the Boy Scouts, which would give him a perfect alibi for the crime. Rader would come up with an excuse to leave the Boy Scout meeting and drive to his parents' house. There he changed into his "hit" clothes, then drove to the Baptist church in

Park City. He would walk from there to the Davis residence and wait outside until she was asleep, then break through the glass door with a cinder block. Delores woke up from the noise, thinking a car had hit her home, to find Rader in the house. Rader told her that he was a wanted man who needed money, food, and a car and that he needed to tie her up. He took her to the bedroom, bound her, and strangled her to death with a pair of pantyhose. He then placed her body in her own car and drove to a lake to hide the body, before he took the car back to her house and wiped off his fingerprints. He also realized that he lost one of his guns, so he entered the residence and found the gun by the patio door that he had broken entering the home. He then went back to his car and returned to the dump site to move the body, finally dumping her under a bridge in Sedgwick County. He changed back into his Scout clothes and returned to camp. The following day he would return to the dump site to take pictures of the body.

The murders would cease and the B.T.K. case descended into the realm of cold cases. By 2004, thirteen years had gone by and there had been nothing but silence from the murderer. It has always been up for debate as to why Rader began writing the media again, after so long. Is it truly because he felt he was being forgotten by history? Or are there other reasons for the emergence from his slumber?

It was March 19th, 2004, when the Wichita Eagle would finally receive a new letter that included Vicki Wegerle's driver's license and several photos of the crime scene. Since Vicki had still been alive and was rushed to the hospital, the police had taken no pictures of the body at the crime scene. It was obvious that the only person that could have these pictures was the killer. The letter was postmarked on March 17th, which was the 27th anniversary of the Shirley Vian murder. It also had a return address with the name Bill Thomas Killman, an obvious reference to B.T.K. After going cold for thirteen years, they knew the killer was still out there. Now the question would become, were there more victims?

On May 5th, 2004, KAKE TV received another letter from B.T.K., that included a word puzzle, a Southwestern Bell employee ID card, and a Wichita school system ID card. In the word puzzle, investigators found many hidden clues about the killer. From this point on, it was obvious that this had become a game to B.T.K. In the word search, he even taunted them with the line "Go for it."

There were several letters found over the next few months, that have still not been released by the police. A letter in June of 2004 was sent directly to the police. On July 17th, 2004, another letter was found at the public library in a mechanical book, the same way the original Otero letter was found. There was some evidence in this letter that would lead the investigators to believe that the killer might have been connected to Wichita State University. He would then send a letter to the police that had a book entitled "The BTK Story." with thirteen chapters:

- A SERIAL KILLER IS BORN
- DAWN
- FETISH
- FANTASY WORLD
- THE SEARCH BEGINS
- HAUNTS
- PJ'S
- MO-ID-RUSE
- HITS
- TREASURED MEMORIES
- FINAL CURTAIN CALL
- DUSK
- WILL THERE BE MORE?

On the thirtieth anniversary of the first letter sent by B.T.K., a suspicious letter was found at a UPS drop box at the OmniCenter. It is believed to be a genuine B.T.K. letter but has never been released to the public.

On November 30th, 2004, in a brilliant move, the police released some of the information that they had gathered about B.T.K. to the public. They knew the killer was watching and would be unable to resist continuing to play the game. They were also hoping that a citizen would recognize this person from the information and provide additional evidence. They released the following statement:

- BTK claims he was born in 1939, which would make him 64 or 65 years old.
- His father died in World War II. His mother and grandparents raised him.
- He has a fascination with railroads and between 1950 to 1955, his mother dated a detective with the railroad.
- In the early 1950s he built and operated a ham radio. He also has knowledge of photography and can develop and print pictures.
- He also likes to hunt, fish, and camp.
- In 1960, BTK claims he went to tech school and then joined the military for active duty and was discharged in 1966 at which time he says he moved back in with his mother.
- He worked repairing copiers and business equipment.
- He admits to soliciting prostitutes.

In December 2004, a white plastic bag wrapped in rubber bands was found in Murdock Park. The bag contained Nancy Fox's driver's license, a letter that had similar chapters to a book from the scene, and other items that may have been taken from the crime scenes. In the letter, they also found a code that would spell out the date of Nancy Fox's murder.

From January to February 2005, several more letters were sent to the media and police, all containing items that were taken from the crime scenes to prove that they were coming directly from the killer. In one of these letters,

B.T.K. would ask if they could trace a floppy disk if he put his writings on it and sent it to them and instructed the police to post their response in the Wichita Eagle. On February 2nd, 2005, the police posted "Rex, it will be ok," and then left a P.O. Box number for him to send his clue. On February 16th, 2005, B.T.K. sent a purple Memorex floppy disk to the police department. The disk was empty, but to Rader's demise, the file that he had deleted was still able to be traced by the police department. They found in the metadata "Christ Lutheran Church" and a file last modified by "Dennis." Upon checking the church's website, they found that Dennis Rader was the president of the church council. The police would then do a drive-by of his house and see a black Jeep Cherokee, and surveillance footage from a Home Depot where B.T.K. left a letter had shown a similar vehicle. Sadly, this was only circumstantial evidence, and they could not move in yet.

The police would obtain a warrant to test the DNA of a pap smear, that was collected to test for cervical cancer, from Rader's twenty-five-year-old daughter, unbeknownst to her. Although there are definite ethical concerns with the police obtaining biological evidence from biological storage, without a person's consent, this is exactly what happened in this case. The DNA evidence would show a familial match to the DNA found under Vicki Wegerle's fingernails, giving the police the evidence they needed to arrest Dennis Rader. On February 25th, 2005, the police pulled over Dennis Rader and arrested him. They would then go on to search his home, vehicle, the church, and the main branch of the public library. In his home, they would seize computer equipment, some black pantyhose from his shed, and a cylindrical container. Just three days later, on the 28th, Rader was charged with ten counts of murder in the first degree. By May 5th, there were rumors that Rader had confessed to all ten murders. Initially, the plea would be entered as not guilty, however, on the scheduled trial date of June 27th, Rader changed his plea to guilty. In that trial, the judge listed off the charges against him and Rader would describe, in detail, the crimes that he committed. Many would say that the matter-of-fact way that Rader described these crimes was an obvious sign of both his callousness and narcissism. On August 18th, 2005, Rader heard the victims' family statements and then gave a thirty-minute monologue apologizing to the families. He would then be sentenced to ten consecutive life sentences, with a minimum of 175 years in prison. At this time, Kansas did not have the death penalty so he would not be sentenced to death. He was eventually transferred to El Dorado Correctional Facility, where he sits today. At the time of this writing, he is seventy-eight years old and if you talk to Dennis he does feel remorse for the victims. He specifically feels remorse for the children and says that if he knew that they were home he would not have gone there. After speaking to my friend Ashleigh, one of Dennis' closest contacts, she explained that Dennis feels that he was born with a devious side of his personality that is always there with him. He now limits his exposure to the things that trigger him in that way.

Myth #1: Dennis Loved to Kill

It is obvious that Rader killed because there was a part of him that enjoyed it. However, was that what really drove him, the killing alone? We know that Rader killed to satisfy a sexual need, but it was not the actual act of sex that drove him. He didn't have sex with any of his victims but would strangle them and then masturbate over the bodies. This obviously constitutes a sexual crime, but with no sexual assault to the bodies we need to look deeper into his psychology to understand what really motivated him to kill.

Although the crimes that Rader committed often didn't go according to plan, he was obsessive about researching his "projects" and meticulously planned out what he was going to do. Even now, Dennis struggles with obsessive-compulsive disorder. He told me that his favorite number is three and he believes that everything relates to threes. His examples to me were "God, Holy Ghost, and Son. Man, Woman, Child. BTK, Crime, Prison. Etc." He also mentioned that he deals with pareidolia, the tendency to perceive specific, often meaningful images in a random pattern. He calls it "monsters off my prison floor." It surprises me that someone that is so obsessive about everything could make so many mistakes in the crimes that he committed. I find it interesting that the unpredictability of these types of situations is what often gets people caught, but Rader seemed to be able to get away with it regardless. Of course, the fact that he started before the advent of DNA research helped him a great deal, but ultimately that would be what got him caught.

Rader would eventually give Katherine Ramsland a matrix that provided fifty-five "projects" listed on it. This matrix had details of the people, their addresses, common movements, and any extra details Rader felt were pertinent to close his "project." Although we know of the ten murders that Rader was convicted of and confessed to, there are many more that he was researching and looking for his "perfect" moment to strike.

The fantasy that Rader was constantly building within himself, was of complete control over these women. Everything that he did would feed his desire to have that control. The danger of stalking them and knowing their every move would be fuel for the event to come. Upon entering the residences, he would hold the families at gunpoint, again controlling every aspect of the situation. His obsession with bondage was another measure of control that would feed that sexual desire of seeing a woman helpless. Finally, he had the ultimate measure of control, controlling life and death itself. This would bring him to his sexual climax and physical release, but he was not finished there. He would then take pictures of his victims, again feeding his need for control over the situation, as he could do anything he wanted with them. To continue feeding his sexual gratification and control, he stole their clothing or put it on at the scene of the crime and took pictures of himself. After the crimes, he taunted the media and police with his letters and packages, all to continue feeling that sense of control. The feeling of danger and the narcissism of believing that you are smarter and better than everyone else would become the ultimate feeling of control.

He enjoyed playing a dangerous game with the police. The delusion that he was the one in control shows his narcissistic personality. He would get excited at the belief that he was pulling all the strings and that they would never catch him. Even when he was arrested for the crimes that he committed, he believed that the police didn't play fair. At that point, he was so lost in his own fantasy, where he was controlling all the pieces on the chessboard, that he couldn't see that it was not a game to the police. They were trying to catch the man who committed all these murders and would go to any lengths to get their man. He may have been toying with them, but they were playing for keeps. Eventually that arrogance would get Rader caught and life imprisonment.

For Rader, it was all about the chase; the murder may have been the apex of the crime, but it was everything that came before and after that really drove him to commit the crimes. The illusion of control and the hunt drove him, the fear and terror that he produced only heightened his desire for more. There is a thin line between being obsessed with killing itself, and being intoxicated by the power and control this gives a person, who feels out of control in the rest of their life. Although Dennis certainly killed for pleasure, it was the control of the situation and the fact that he seemed to be getting away with it that really satisfied his desires.

Myth #2: Dennis Had More than 10 Victims

We know that Rader admitted to killing ten people and went into great detail about those crimes. We also know that Rader had a list of over fifty-five "projects" that he planned to kill. Does that mean that there were more victims? What did he do in those thirteen years of silence? Was it truly that he was so busy with his regular life that he just stopped killing?

Rader is unique in terms of serial killers. Often serial killers will ramp up their crimes, eventually continuing to kill in faster and faster succession. The cooling-off periods will become shorter and less predictable and they will often get into a state of frenzy. In Dahmer's case, in the end, he was killing every few days and sometimes even closer together than that. Rader would sometimes go years between kills and killed in three different decades. He killed seven in the 1970s, although we know that he attempted more. He waited six years before killing again in 1985 when he would kill two. Then five years later he killed his final known victim in 1991. Then, silence for thirteen years.

So, what happened in those moments of silence? The years between some of the murders? In some interviews, Dennis suggested that having a family and changing jobs kept him too busy to properly stalk his "projects." It is interesting that he used the term "project" to depersonalize his victims. This would effectively allow him to "cube" his life. "Cubing" would be a term that Dennis would coin for the way that he was able to live in several realities at once, without them intersecting. He also mentioned that during that time he would have "motel parties," which he believed controlled some of his desires to kill women. During these "motel parties," Dennis would bring photos that he had taken at the crime scenes, clothing that he had stolen from his victims, and various bondage and sex toys. He would spend his time tying himself in bondage and taking pictures of himself using a camera that he rigged to be able to take a picture by using a squeeze ball and tube. He would then masturbate while in the bondage to satisfy his sexual desires. He would also wear masks that would allow him to fully realize his fantasies of being a woman in bondage and distress.

Katherine Ramsland writes in her book, *Confessions of a Serial Killer*, that Dennis never stopped looking for victims. Even in the years that he was silent, he was constantly stalking and working on his "projects." She believes that the only reason that he may not have offended during that time was his lack of time. During his breaks from murdering, Dennis was a family man, church member, scout leader, and employee. This would leave him little time to find the "perfect" conditions to commit the crimes that he liked to commit. Rader revealed to the police in 2005 that he was already stalking an eleventh victim and had even tried to fulfill the fantasy but was thwarted. He would have certainly finished the job if the opportunity had arisen.

Dennis Rader and B.T.K. hit the news again on August 22nd, 2023, eighteen years after his arrest, when the police conducted their second search on the former property of Dennis Rader in Park City, Kansas. They had previously searched the property in April and had found several items of interest, including pantyhose tied in a configuration to bind a person, chains believed to be used in bondage, and several other items not released to the public. These items bring up the possibility of Rader's involvement in several cold cases that have never been attributed to B.T.K. At least two cold cases of kidnappings that are under investigation list Dennis as the prime suspect. Dennis' daughter was even brought in on the task force to see if she could have enough influence to get Rader to speak about the crimes. So far, Dennis has denied any involvement in any other murders or kidnappings. Only time will tell if there is any real evidence to be found to connect Rader to these cold cases but, so far, he has only been charged and convicted of the ten murders that he has confessed to.

Myth #3: Dennis Started Writing Again Because He Wanted to Be Infamous

After the murder of Dolores Davis in 1991, no one had heard anything from B.T.K. until the first letter in 2004. He likely continued to stalk new "projects" throughout those thirteen years and may have killed more people that we have no knowledge of. Why would Rader suddenly begin to write to the police and media again, after thirteen years of silence? Some people believe that he felt like he was being forgotten, so he couldn't help himself. Others believe that he felt like he never got the credit that he deserved and was angry about not being recognized along with the likes of Bundy and Dahmer.

Rader was a student of the game and studied other serial killers. His favorite killer to study was H.H. Holmes, because of the way that he built the murder castle to trap, torture, and kill. Although it was not done by design, Dennis even mentioned to me that upon seeing the cover of this book, he was glad to be next to his favorite killer. Rader even dreamed of creating his own murder castle. I am sure he also took notice of other killers and felt that he was better than any of them since at the time he was the only one that hadn't been caught. You would think that he was flying high at the thought of not even being a suspect in the ten murders that he had committed, for almost thirty years running. However, this could never be the case for Rader.

In 2004, the police had no real leads at all. They had DNA evidence from several of the crime scenes but with no matches to anyone. They also had victim statements but no leads or positive identification. That would all change when the communications from B.T.K. started again. Rader would have gotten away with 10+ counts of first-degree murder if he had just stayed silent. Thankfully for the families, they would have some closure when the man responsible would finally be caught in less than a year after resurfacing.

I happen to be good friends with Ashleigh Keto, who is the closest friend that Dennis has had since he has been in prison. Before 2020 and the COVID pandemic, she regularly visited him in person at El Dorado Correctional Facility and still talks to him on the phone several times a week. Because of my friendship with Ashleigh, I have had the unique opportunity to ask questions for this book to get answers from Dennis himself. I had a few questions that I wanted to know the answers directly from the source. First, I wanted to know why he decided to begin writing again after being silent for so long. Dennis confirmed that it was the story published in the Wichita Eagle on the thirtieth anniversary of the Otero murders in 2004 that forced him to set the record straight. The news article also mentioned an attorney who was working on a book about the unsolved B.T.K. murders. The book would cover seven of the known murders linked to B.T.K. In the article, they would say that they believed that the B.T.K. strangler was either dead or in prison. This lit a fire under Dennis, as he felt that he had to preserve his legacy; this would prove to be his final mistake.

We have already established that Rader is an extreme narcissist and has a deep need for recognition for his crimes. When you look at the letters during this time, you see that Rader is presenting his own book and releasing chapter titles, in his attempt to tell his story. This led him into an intoxicating "game" with the police. It had been years since he had played the "game," and the article reignited that desire. He was older and his children were grown, so he had the time to really play the "game" the way that he wanted, feeding his need for danger and control. As he started writing these letters and dropping off packages, Rader started to feel a kinship with the lead investigator, Lieutenant Ken Landwehr. This deluded relationship with the investigator would feed his grandiose personality and lead him to believe that he was always several steps ahead of the police. It was his arrogance that kept him talking. For the first time in twenty-five years, B.T.K. was back in the news and everyone was talking about the killer being back. Rader would be buzzing and living in a constant high from all the attention that would only feed his narcissistic personality.

So, did he start writing again to become infamous? Not really. He started writing again because he wanted to make sure they got his legacy correct. He wanted to be the one who was in control of the B.T.K. story, not some attorney who didn't even know all of the crimes that had been committed. This led to a different sort of narcissism for Rader, to the cat and mouse game that he believed he was playing with the police, where he thought that they were having as much fun as he was. This deluded thinking is exactly what would get him caught in just a few months' time.

Legend: Dennis was the Zodiac Killer

When I spoke with Ashleigh, I wanted her to ask Dennis what he thought I should include in a book about Myths & Legends regarding him. He responded that he had been questioned multiple times regarding the unidentified Zodiac Killer case. When I was writing the chapter on the Zodiac for this book, I was not aware that B.T.K. was also a suspect in the case. I personally had not investigated the possibility, until now, however, there are many people that believe that there is lots of circumstantial evidence that points towards Rader also being Zodiac. There is even a book written by a retired detective, Kimberely McGath, called *Zodiac: Settling the Score*, which provides all the evidence for Rader being the Zodiac.

As a detective, Kimberely McGath had a bachelor's degree in psychology and eventually ended up in the cold case division of her police department. As a rookie detective, she was instrumental in closing a cold case and finding the remains of a missing victim. She also closed the case made famous by Truman Capote's book, *In Cold Blood*, identifying Richard Hickock and Perry Smith as the killers. However, she did not even run across the Zodiac case until 2014, while attending a presentation on the serial killer at a cold case seminar. Immediately, she recognized the modus operandi and knew that the killer must be Dennis Rader.

During the time of the Zodiac murders, Rader was serving in the United States Air Force from 1966-1970. He started basic training in Texas and later served in Okinawa and Tokyo. To me, this information would disqualify him from being the Zodiac. However, Kimberely makes a case for murders in 1963, that were suspected Zodiac murders, that could be attributed to Rader. She also cites a conversation that Rader had with an FBI agent, where Rader would say that he traveled a lot during that period and that he was "free to kill." She says that Rader mentioned that he murdered more during this time than when he was in Kansas, also opening the possibility that Rader killed while he was living overseas. Kimberely says that Rader admitted to fantasizing about kidnapping and killing Annette Funicello, because of the movie trailer for *Muscle Beach Party*. In the trailer, Annette and Frankie Avalon are seen scantily clad on the beach. She supposes that this enraged Rader, and he was compelled to act. There is some weight to this theory since a young couple was killed shortly after, just north of where the film was being shot.

In her book, she also theorized that Zodiac was also photographing his crime scenes, just like Rader did later in his crimes. She also mentioned many other parallels between the Zodiac and Rader, including:
- They both used a taxi during one of the murders.
  - In the Zodiac case, he was riding in a taxi and killed the taxi driver.
  - In Rader's case, he would ride in a taxi on the way to commit some of his known murders.
- They both sent letters to the police, media, and family members, which were typed or handwritten.
- They both carried the same weapons, in the same manner. They carried multiple guns in holsters, precut bondage materials, and knives.
- They both called the police to report their murders and left the receivers off the hook.
- They both used ciphers and codes in their communication with police and the media.

- They both instructed their female victims to bind their male victims.
- Victims from both killers would describe their captors as nervous or "shaking."
- They both would tell their victims that they were a wanted man, just needed money, and a vehicle.
- They both wrote their page numbers the same, used identical abbreviations, and used the same phrases in their letters.
- They both adapted folk songs to poetry, spent time at libraries, and referenced history.

McGath also touched on the people who believe that the Zodiac was not a sexual sadist like Rader is. Although the Zodiac seemed to not have any sexual element to his killings, he certainly discussed his fantasies about torture and killing which he enjoyed even more than sex. I have already established that Rader, although definitely a sexual sadist, was more fulfilled by stalking, terror, and bondage rather than sex and murder. For Rader, murder was just the climax of the event. Does this mean that they are the same person?

When I look at this circumstantial "evidence" that could potentially link Zodiac and Rader, all I see is similarity. I believe that killers can often have similarities in motive, design, and methods, but this does not mean that they are the same person. When I read that Rader was, more than likely, not even in the country when some of the Zodiac murders happened, it became an impossibility for me that they were the same. However, I do understand that Rader would often study those who had come before him and the Zodiac killer was big news, as well as one of the rare killers who had also not been caught. Another aspect that leads me to believe that they could not have been the same person, is the fact that Rader returned to set the record straight and cement his legacy. This exact same speculation was happening in the Zodiac case during Rader's known active killing period. If he was the Zodiac, why would Rader have never tried to set that record straight? We know that he was unable to allow the police to get the facts wrong, so why would he allow it to go for so long with no real manifesto or communication to let the real crimes be known? For me, it seems implausible that Rader is the Zodiac. I think he may have emulated the Zodiac and used some of his M.O. to bolster his own because it had worked, but we are still guessing as to who the Zodiac is. Dennis himself would chuckle at the ascertainment that he could be the Zodiac but gave me no indication if it was true or not. However, I am sure that being talked about in the same sentence as one of the most enduring criminal cases in history is something that does nothing more than stroke his ego.

Expand Your Mind

Podcasts

- *Murder Metal Mayhem* - Ep. 81 – "Dennis Rader: Bind Torture Kill"
- *TimeSuck w/ Dan Cummins* - Ep. 63 – "BTK Killer: Bind. Torture. Kill."
- *Last Podcast on the Left* - Eps. 59 & 61

Books

- *Confessions of a Serial Killer: The Untold Story of Dennis Rader, the BTK Killer* by Katherine Ramsland
- *Inside the Mind of BTK* by John Douglas
- *A Serial Killer's Daughter* by Kerri Rawson

Documentaries & Movies

- *BTK: Confessions of a Serial Killer* (2022)
- *BTK: Chasing a Serial Killer* (2020)

BIBLIOGRAPHY

Chapter 1: Elizabeth Bathory

Borowski, J., dir. *Serial Killer Culture TV*. Season 2, Episode 4, "Infamous Bathory." Waterfront Productions, 2018.

Kettler, S. "Elizabeth Bathory. Biography." October 3, 2023. www.biography.com/crime/elizabeth-bathory.

Littlechild, C. "Elizabeth Bathory Would Bathe In Blood?" Ripley's, January 12, 2023. www.ripleys.com/weird-news/elizabeth-bathory-and-bathing-in-blood.

Sherman, E.. "Meet Elizabeth Bathory, The 'Blood Countess' Who May Have Been History's Most Prolific Serial Killer." Allthatsinteresting.com. www.allthatsinteresting.com/elizabeth-bathory.

Michael Newton. *The Encyclopedia of Serial Killers*. Checkmark Books, 2000.

Chapter 2: Jack the Ripper

Aabech, B. dir. (*Jack the Ripper: London's Most Notorious Killer.* Entertain Me Productions, 2020.

"Casebook: Jack the Ripper Suspects." Casebook, accessed December 13, 2023. ww.casebook.org/suspects/jill.html.

Little, B. "A Surprising New Theory About Jack the Ripper's Victims." Aetv.com, April 8, 2019. www.aetv.com/real-crime/vicitms-of-jack-the-ripper-new-theory.

Michael Newton, *The Encyclopedia of Serial Killers*. Checkmark Books, 2000.

Skinner, K. & Stewart, E. *The Ultimate Jack the Ripper Sourcebook*. Robinson Publishing, 2000.

Thejacktherippertour.com. "Jack the Ripper Victims." Accessed December 12, 2023. www.thejacktherippertour.com/casebook/victims.

Thejacktherippertour.com. "Jack the Ripper Suspects." Accessed December 12, 2023. www.thejacktherippertour.com/casebook/suspects/.

Whitechapeljack.com. ("Jack the Ripper Suspects." Accessed December 12, 2023. www.whitechapeljack.com/jack-the-ripper-suspects.

Chapter 3: Herman W. Mudgett

Baillie, K. "Did serial killer H.H. Holmes fake his own death?" May 22, 2018. www.penntoday.upenn.edu/news/did-serial-killer-h-h-holmes-fake-his-own-death.

Borowski, J. dir. *H.H. Holmes: America's First Serial Killer.* Waterfront Productions, 2004.

Crimeandinvestigation.co.uk. (2023, Dec 13). Could Jack the Ripper Have Been HH Holmes? www.crimeandinvestigation.co.uk/shows/american-ripper-in-london/could-jack-the-ripper-have-been-hh-holmes-.

Killelea, E. (2017, May 4). Serial Killer H.H. Holmes' Body Exhumed: What We Know. Rolling Stone Magazine. www.rollingstone.com/culture/culture-news/serial-killer-h-h-holmes-body-exhumed-what-we-know-126699/.

Little, B. (2020, Jan 23). Did Serial Killer H.H. Holmes Really Build a 'Murder Castle'? History.com. www.history.com/news/murder-castle-h-h-holmes-chicago.

Newton, M. (2000). The Encyclopedia of Serial Killers. Checkmark Books.

Ostrom, M. (Producer). (2017). American Ripper. [Documentary]. Magilla Entertainment.

Runnells, C. (2023, Feb 24). Was Serial Killer H.H. Holmes also Jack the Ripper? His relative makes a case in Fort Myers. Fort Myers News-Press. www.news-press.com/story/life/2023/02/24/serial-killer-jack-the-ripper-and-hh-holmes-the-same-person-american-monster/69924371007/.

Schechter, H. (2008). Depraved: The Definitive True Story of H.H. Holmes, Whose Grotesque Crimes Shattered Turn-of-the-Century Chicago. Gallery Books.

Chapter 4: Lizzie Borden

Alexander, K. (2023, Oct). Lizzie Borden - Killer of Fall River Massachusetts? Legends of America. www.legendsofamerica.com/lizzie-borden/.

Anderson, E. (2019, Sept 20). Lizzie Borden's LGBTQ Secret. Medium. www.authoredanderson.medium.com/lizzie-bordens-lgbtq-secret-b405b014a50f.

Chapman, S. (2018, July 6). Lizzie and the Tilden-Thurber Incident. The Hatchet. www.lizzieandrewborden.com/HatchetOnline/lizzie-and-the-tilden-thurber-incident.html.

Ghost Guide Daniel. (2023, Dec 13). Lizzie Borden House…Stay Overnight in Dark History. GhostWalks.

com. www.ghostwalks.com/articles/lizzie-borden-house-ghost-stories.

Groff, N. (Director). (2011). Ghost Adventures Season 5 Episode 5: Lizzie Borden House. [TV Series]. Travel Channel.

Hardwick, C. (2022, Feb 28). Was Lizzie Borden Really a Lesbian? IN Magazine. www.inmagazine.ca/2022/02/queer-crime-was-lizzie-borden-really-a-lesbian/.

Medeiros, D. (2021, Oct 26). The Lizzie Borden House Was Named as One of the World's Best Haunted Hotels. How Scary is It? The Herald News. www.heraldnews.com/story/lifestyle/travel/2021/10/26/lizzie-borden-house-fall-river-best-haunted-hotel-ghost-paranormal/8546497002/.

Yuko, E. (2016, Aug 4). Lizzie Borden: Why a 19th-Century Axe Murderer Still Fascinates Us. Rolling Stone Magazine. www.rollingstone.com/culture/culture-features/lizzie-borden-why-a-19th-century-axe-murder-still-fascinates-us-250467/.

Chapter 5: Ed Gein

Bartle, T. (2022, Dec 30). 13 Horror Movies Inspired by Serial Killer Ed Gein. CreepyCatalog.com. https://creepycatalog.com/horror.movies-inspired-by-serial-killer-ed-gein/.

Borowski, J. (2016). The Ed Gein File: A Psycho's Confession and Case Documents. Waterfront Productions.

Daniels, R. (2022, July 13). Ed Gein: The Cannibal Myth Exposed. RobertCDaniels.com. http://robertcdaniels.com/ed_gein.htm.

Day, J. (Director) (2023) Psycho: The Lost Tapes of Ed Gein [Documentary]. Pyramid Productions.

Fraga, K. (2022, Jan 29) The Macabre Story of Ed Gein, The Serial Killer That Used Human Body Parts to Make Furniture. Allthatsinteresting.com. https://allthatsinteresting.com/ed-gein.

Grieve-Smith, A. (2016, April 11). Owning Ed Gein. Trans Blog. https://transblog.grieve-smith.com/2016/04/11/owning-ed-gein/.

Newton, M. (2000). The Encyclopedia of Serial Killers. Checkmark Books.

Piccotti, T. (2023, Nov 27) Ed Gein. Biography.com. https://www.biography.com/crime/ed-gein.

Schechter, H. (1998). Deviant: The Shocking True Story of Ed Gein, the Original Psycho. Gallery Books.

Chapter 6: The Zodiac

Butterfield, M. (2023, Dec 15). ZodiacKillerFacts.com. https://zodiackillerfacts.com/zodiac-letters/.

CharlesManson.com (2023, Dec 15). The Zodiac / Manson Conspiracy. https://www.charlesmanson.com/theories/zodiac-manson-conspiracy/.

Davidson, K. (Director). (2020). The Most Dangerous Animal of All [Documentary] FX Studios.

Davis, H. (1997). The Zodiac Manson Connection. Howard Davis.

Felton, J. (2021, Dec 28). FBI Confirms Zodiac Killer's Infamous 340 Cipher Has Been Decoded, and His Message Finally Revealed. IFLScience.com. https://www.iflscience.com/fbi-confirms-zodiac-killers-infamous-340-cipher-has-been-decoded-and-his-message-finally-revealed-62044.

Newton, M. (2000). The Encyclopedia of Serial Killers. Checkmark Books.

Nock, A. (Director). (2023). Myth of the Zodiac Killer [Documentary]. Texas Crew Productions.

Voigt, T. (1998, March 20). ZodiacKiller.com. https://zodiackiller.com/zodiac-killer-suspects/.

Voigt, T. (1998, March 20). ZodiacKiller.com. https://zodiackiller.com/zodiac-killer-victims/.

Chapter 7: John Wayne Gacy

Blackhurst, R. (2021). John Wayne Gacy: Devil in Disguise [Documentary]. NBC News Studios.

Borowski, J. (2020). John Wayne Gacy Hunting a Predator: The Pursuit, Arrest, and Confession. Waterfront Productions.

Dorsch, W. (2023). Omnipotent: Don't Ask Don't Tell. BOWKER.

Motta, B. (Creator). (2021, April 29). The Gacy Tapes (#1-33) [Audio Podcast]. Defense Diaries. Spotify. https://open.spotify.com/show/0duAplGAfvbaGmC6IVYxAh.

Newton, M. (2000). The Encyclopedia of Serial Killers. Checkmark Books.

Stanley, J. (2019, Jan 1). Evil Lives Here Season 5 Episode 1: You Know My Brother's Name [Documentary].

Tron, G. (2021, March 25). 'Smelled Like a Morgue!' The Brazen (And Stupid) Way That John Wayne Gacy Got Caught. Oxygen True Crime. https://www.oxygen.com/true-crime-buzz/the-brazen-way-that-serical-killer-john-wayne-gacy-got-caught.

Chapter 8: Ted Bundy

Berlinger, J. (Creator). (2019). Conversations with a Killer: The Ted Bundy Tapes. RadicalMedia.

FBI.gov. (2023, Dec 16). Ted Bundy. https://vault.fbi.gov/Ted%20Bundy%20.

Hammon, E.J. & Richards, F. (2022). Ted Bundy: Memories of the Beast. Grim Reality Publishing.

Hammon, E.J. (2016, Sept 11). Bundy's Father Figures. BundyPhile.com. https://bundyphile.com/2016/09/11/bundys-father-figures/.

Hammon, E.J. (2013, Dec 29) Ted's Relationship with Women. BundyPhile.com. https://bundyphile.com/2013/12/29/teds-relationship-with-women/.

Hammon, E.J. (2019, Aug 3). Did Ted Bundy Want to Get Caught? BundyPhile.com. https://bundyphile.com/2019/03/08/did-ted-bundy-want-to-get-caught/.

Hammon, E.J. (2023, Oct 16). Bundy's Unsuccessful Escape Attempts. BundyPhile.com. https://bundyphile.com/2023/10/16/bundys-unsuccessful-escape-attempts/.

Hammon, E.J. (2019, Aug 20). Ted Bundy: Did He Abduct Singer Debbie Harry? BundyPhile.com. https://bundyphile.com/2019/08/20/ted-bundy-did-he-abduct-singer-debbie-harry/.

Holt, C. (Director). (2019). Ted Bundy: Mind of a Monster [Documentary]. Arrow Media.

Newton, M. (2000). The Encyclopedia of Serial Killers. Checkmark Books.

Rule, A. (2008). The Stranger Beside Me. Pocket Books.

Yang, A. (2019, Feb 15). Timeline of Many of Ted Bundy's Brutal Crimes. ABC News. https://abcnews.

go.com/US/timeline-ted-bundys-brutal-crimes/story?id=61077236.

Chapter 9: Jeffrey Dahmer

ABC News. (2017, Aug 10). Decades Later, New Clues in a Cold Case. ABC News. https://abcnews.go.com/Primetime/story?id=3466806&page=1.

Berlinger, J. (Creator). (2022). Conversations with a Killer: The Jeffrey Dahmer Tapes. RadicalMedia.

Borowski, J. (2017). Dahmer's Confession: The Milwaukee Cannibal's Arrest. Waterfront Productions.

Dahmer, L. (1994). A Father's Story. William Morrow and Company, Inc.

Holt, C. (Director). (2020). Jeffrey Dahmer: Mind of a Monster [Documentary]. Arrow Media.

Hurley, B. (2022, Oct 4). Did Jeffrey Dahmer Kill the Son of America's Most Wanted Host John Walsh? Independent.com. https://www.the-independent.com/news/world/americas/crime/adam-walsh-killer-john-son-jeffrey-dahmer-b2194793.html.

James, T. (2022). Dahmer - The Psych Reports: The complete psychiatric examination of the Milwaukee Cannibal. Serial Pleasures Publishing.

King-Carroll, K. (2022, Oct 11). Racism and Homophobia enabled Jeffrey Dahmer's Crimes. The Washington Post. https://www.washingtonpost.com/made-by-history/2022/10/11/racism-homophobia-enabled-jeffrey-dahmers-crimes/.

Mendoza, J. (2022, Sept 22). The Chilling Way Alcohol Tied into Jeffrey Dahmer's Murders. Grunge.com. https://www.grunge.com/1017767/the-chilling-way-alcohol-tied-into-jeffrey-dahmers-murders/.

Oxygen True Crime. (2017, Nov 12). Dahmer on Dahmer: Class Clown - Bonus Clip [Documentary]. YouTube. https://www.youtube.com/watch?v=e9IieRn96to.

Smith, J. (1992, Feb 12). Psychiatrist Says Dahmer Needed Alcohol Before He Could Kill. UPI.com. https://www.upi.com/Archives/1992/02/12/Psychiatrist-says-Dahmer-needed-alcohol-before-he-could-kill/1669697870800/.

Chapter 10: Dennis Rader

Beeman, A. (2023, Jan 6). Inside Dennis Rader's Childhood: What Made Him the BTK Killer? Heavy.com. https://heavy.com/entertainment/2020/09/inside-dennis-raders-childhood-btk-killer/.

Bonn, S. (2019, Feb 18). Inside the Mind of Dennis Rader, AKA BTK. Psychology Today. https://www.psychologytoday.com/us/blog/wicked-deeds/201902/inside-the-mind-serial-killer-dennis-rader-aka-btk.

Cavallier, A. (2023, Sept. 1). BTK Killer Dennis Rader is Potentially Linked to Five New Murders, Daughter Says. Independent.com. https://www.the-independent.com/news/world/americas/crime/btk-killer-dennis-rader-kerri-rawson-b2401889.html.

Childs, C. (2022). BTK: Confessions of a Serial Killer [Documentary]. Wolf Entertainment.

Colletta, S. (2023, Dec 16). Who is the Zodiac Killer? https://www.suecoletta.com/who-is-the-zodiac/.

Douglas, J. (2008). Inside the Mind of BTK: The True Story Behind the Thirty-Year Hunt for the Notorious Wichita Serial Killer. Jossey-Bass.

Hirschfield, J. (2019). BTK: A Killer Among Us [Documentary]. Cream Productions.

McGath, K. (2015). Zodiac: Settling the Score. CreateSpace.

Ramsland, K. (2016). Confessions of a Serial Killer: The Untold Story of Dennis Rader, the BTK Killer. ForeEdge.

FINAL THOUGHTS

John Wayne Gacy would famously say, "…the dead won't bother you, it's the living you have to worry about." I have always believed that the pursuit of studying true crime, as well as the reasons and methods of these killers, is a worthy pursuit. There are some people out there who find it macabre. They often choose to place their heads in the sand and pretend that it never happened. I believe this is a mistake, the truth that humanity will always find a reason to kill each other continues to be as present in our time as it ever was. We live under a constant threat of our total destruction and with the advent of the internet, instant news coverage, and TikTok we have an ever-available source of information. This makes watching true crime little different from watching the nightly news.

There is a belief that studying, discussing, and creating products around true crime figures is glorifying the killer. I would suggest that it all depends on intent. There are certainly people out there who take it way too far and glorify these people as heroes. However, I believe it is vitally important to never forget history. These people have become part of our collective history, and it becomes dangerous to not understand the reasons and methods that these people use to kill. If we can remain aware of how these people behave and interact, not only can we be safer as a society, but we can also prevent these types of crimes from happening. This is something that would take a monumental effort from lots of psychotherapy to places to house offenders who are not able to be rehabilitated. Just like everything else, there are never any simple answers. But ignoring these people and sweeping everything under the carpet never helps anyone. Often it is the apathy and turning a blind eye that creates many of these situations.

I often hear that true crime is "hot" right now, it is just a fad. The interest in serial killers is at an all-time high. The truth is that it has always been popular. After the death of Elizabeth Bathory people have collected rocks from her castles to keep as mementos for hundreds of years. The history books are filled with wars, death, and popular events that have kept people fascinated for hundreds of years. The only difference that we have now is that all the information is readily available for all to see. This is the first time in history where we truly have a global community, where you can post one TikTok video, and people from around the world can view, like, and share. True crime has always been of interest to people and will always be of interest. We all want to know why people do what they do. How could someone, that seems so normal, do the horrific things that these killers have done? Just to get a little more personal, we all want to understand why we have some of those dark feelings ourselves. There are times when all of us have fantasized about harming another person. It is not a unique thought and those thoughts do not make us a monster. However, this leaves us all fascinated to know more.

The endeavor of writing this book started from my obsession with true crime and has led me down a path that keeps me hungry for more. The overarching theme of the series is to show people that true crime incorporates all of crime. It is not just serial killers, but a larger world. I intended for this to be part one of a three-part book. However, instead, we are only scratching the surface with volume one of a three-volume set. I am aware that even this volume is far from exhaustive. There are many other theories and ideas that deserve to be focused on, but time and space are always limiting. This may be the first volume of three but there will always be room to expand. As I chose the serial killers for this volume, I wanted to pick the killers that most people were familiar with but may have not seen some of the myths and legends that have grown around them. In further editions, I envision adding new serial killers to the list, as well as revisiting myths that I have not covered in this edition.

The next volume of this collection will cover another aspect of true crime and focus on criminals. One of my first loves was the mafia. As a child, I studied the biographies of many mob figures and had an idealized version of the mob. They only killed other mobsters and they had a code that they lived by. If you were a rat, you died. The romanticism of the mafia would be at its height during the late 80s and 90s, just when I was growing up. *The Godfather* and *The Sopranos* would fuel our love for the gangster movie. It is another aspect of true crime that has not only permeated our minds but also our pop culture. In this volume, we will follow the same formula and discuss the history of the criminal three myths about them, and a legend that has arisen because of them. I hope you are as excited about this as I am.

I am currently sitting here writing this last paragraph and we are closing out the year 2023. In the new year of 2024, I will be releasing this book which is the first of many. I will be doing a convention tour where I will be speaking and selling my products. I will have the opportunity and pleasure of meeting many of you. I hope that you will share your stories with me and updates on myths and legends you have heard or believe that I should cover. This series is a living breathing document, that with new forensics could change drastically. I am always game to find the most up-to-date and current research on the subject. I hope that you

have enjoyed this first volume and will continue swimming
in those deep waters with me.

Still in the deep waters,
Jeff Ignatowski

For more news about Jeff Ignatowski, subscribe
to our newsletter at *wbp.bz/newsletter*.

Word-of-mouth is critical to an author's long-term
success. If you appreciated this book, please leave a
review on the Amazon sales page at *wbp.bz/beyond*.

www.ingramcontent.com/pod-product-compliance
Lightning Source LLC
Chambersburg PA
CBHW070418310726
48977CB00003B/742